THE CHAPLET OF PEARLS

THE CHAPLET
OF PEARLS

HARRIET WAUGH

BLOOMSBURY

Grateful acknowledgement is made to Reed Consumer Books Ltd for permission to reprint lines from 'Noise by Pooh' from *The House at Pooh Corner* by A. A. Milne, published by Methuen Children's Books.

First published 1997

Bloomsbury Publishing Plc, 38 Soho Square; London WIV 5DF

A CIP catalogue record for this book
is available from the British Library

ISBN O 7475 3280 X

10 9 8 7 6 5 4 3 2 1

Typeset by Hewer Text Composition Services, Edinburgh
Printed in Great Britain by Clays Ltd, St Ives plc

FOR RICHARD

'Stay', quoth Reputation,
'Do not forsake me; for it is my nature
If once I part from any man I meet
I am never found again.'

John Webster, *The Duchess of Malfi*
Act III Scene II

Chapter One

She was standing before her bathroom mirror putting on make-up. For someone who did not believe in delighting men and had not as yet made up her mind to delight women, Hilary Greep took considerable pleasure in subtly highlighting her large dull grey eyes. At twenty-five she was very pretty, with mouse-brown hair that lay like a helmet round her demure features. Everything about her was understated and yet said 'Here I am'. She wore a shapeless calf-length blue dress which, like all her clothes, hung loose. She hated anything that restricted her waist or called attention to her size 32B breasts. Now, putting on her round gold-rimmed metal spectacles, she inspected her image in the glass, saw it was androgynous, and was satisfied. She was alone in this perception. Others saw her as soft and as feminine as tissue paper.

Her bed-sitting-room was a mess. Books, half-empty mugs, half a banana on a plate and a cat lay on the floor around the double futon, which she now rolled up as a gesture to tidiness. Lovingly, she gave Alistair some milk and cat food. The only other piece of furniture was a large plywood desk covered with books and papers. On the white walls four particularly gloomy posters of the work of Edvard Munch glared out. For Hilary, the studio flat was a nun's cell. Her friends considered it a dirty scruffy pad.

She collected her writing utensils and eight books which she put into a canvas bag. Then, leaving the flat, she started on the journey from Shepherd's Bush to the London Library.

Katherine Sackville sat at her desk writing letters. Her five Pekinese snored, huddled together in two picturesque groups by her chair. She was so used to their snuffling ways that she never heard them. She was very thin and tall with button features and large round eyes of electric blue, and natural-looking brown curly hair. Large Victorian rings with complicated settings and dark stones clicked on her long thin fingers. She spent a good deal of money on shoes that seemed to shorten her narrow feet and favoured highly patterned dark dresses of light wool, always referred to as 'frocks', over which she sometimes wore a cardigan in winter. From her appearance, there was no guessing her age, although *Who's Who* stated that she was seventy-five. Twenty years before she had retired early from being headmistress of one of the country's top academic private day schools for girls. Soon afterwards she was created a baroness and took her place in the House of Lords. Until lately she had sat on an endless succession of commissions on such diverse subjects as Ethics in Science, Drainage in Morton-on-Sea (this was after an aberrant outbreak of typhus in the town) and the feasibility of a fourth international airport in Hertfordshire. On committees she made an extremely effective chair.

Now she only chaired The Chaplet of Pearls, an informal discussion group which met twice a year to discuss the works of the Victorian writer, Charlotte M. Yonge. It was in this capacity that she was writing to Moira Lockheart at her villa on the island of Saint-Barthélemy in the West Indies. Katherine went to stay with Moira on an average of once every three years, ever since Moira built the house twenty-five years ago. In those days it had been quite a discovery. No hotels, no West Indians sweeping floors and making you feel guilty for reducing them to a servicing class. Just good French food, wonderful sand, bougainvillaea, palm trees and mountains. Despite the new hotels, the sodden state that Moira got into most evenings and rather more tourists than in the past, it was still wonderful.

Dear Moira [she wrote],

I have done something rather clever. The Literature Society has consented to a lecture on the life and works of Charlotte M. Yonge on March 26th! I want you to give it. You must. We Pearls are all getting old and this might be our last chance to infect a different generation with our enthusiasm. If there is a positive response to the lecture, I think when we have our meeting of The Chaplet of Pearls on the 30th we should discuss the possibility of allowing new members to join our group. As usual that meeting will take place at Grace's, even though she has had the ill nature to move to a poky little house behind Notting Hill Gate. I have sent her Percy to 'do' for her as she no longer has any servants, but Grace complains about her drinking.

Grace left South Audley Street after Robert's stroke. She tells me he's a vegetable in the London Clinic. Poor Blanche is in a similar state at the Royal Free Hospital. It was Christmas that did *her* in.

There will be only six of us at the meeting of The

Chaplet of Pearls. Good Annabel is in the lotus position somewhere high up in the Himalayas, while Bad Annabel may be too ill to come. I fear she only has a short time left. Perhaps a mercy. She is very thin and takes only pink fluidy things, although she adores being brought smoked salmon and so forth. She says it quickens her senses. You still feel it's she who's entertaining you rather than you her. You will see her, won't you, when you come? She looks forward to visits, or at least I think she does.

Not all is death, gloom and decay but I cannot think of anything positive about life at the moment. Moira, if by any chance your skin is flaking, your teeth are soft in their gums (or have you had them all out? Most of mine are still here!) and your limbs are weighted as if against a current of water, please, please, don't mention it to me. I do not *feel* for my friends. I want to be young with the sap rising and not to know the likes of us.

Look forward to seeing you. Don't let us down.

Love, Katherine

Katherine put down her pen and looked affectionately at the curled and entwined bodies of the dogs. 'Walkies,' she said.

They leapt to their feet and ran up and down the room.

Katherine lived in a flat in Camden Hill Road. The large, high-ceilinged sitting-room in which she worked was painted yellow, with deep armchairs covered in terracotta cotton and a large sofa in burnished yellow silk. The walls were covered in eighteenth- and nineteenth-century water-colours. Together with her husband Kenneth, who had died four years earlier, she had spent the middle years of her marriage rummaging

4

and scrummaging around picture galleries and had built up, for comparatively little money, an impressive collection.

Going out was a time-consuming business. The day beyond the window looked murky and uninviting. Katherine went to her bedroom (a light, white room dominated by an elaborately carved double bed), and changed her cardigan for a thicker, heavier one. Then she went to the cupboard in the hall for her black wool coat and wound a long mauve scarf round her neck. Next there were the leads and the dogs. Brahms was particularly naughty, darting forward and back and shaking his head just as she nearly succeeded in attaching the metal clip to his collar. Thoroughly exhausted, she set the alarm, shoved and pulled the five dogs out of the flat, double-locked all three locks on her front door, and set forth with Mozart, Brahms, M. Yonge, Rossetti and Browning for Kensington Gardens.

Moira, already in England, was not to receive Katherine's letter for several months. That day she was in the London Library pretending to do research for a book on the flora and fauna of the French Caribbean island of Saint-Barthélemy.

Moira was a writer of historical novels. Her last had appeared three years ago. Since then she had only been pretending to write. She was very proud of having all her faculties and liked to arrange meetings at the Library with journalists sent to interview her. She would then make them carry her bag of books to some new restaurant which had opened since her last visit to England. Eating was a passion with her. In old age she was plump with pendulous breasts, her blunt features disappearing into the soft folds of her short neck. She enjoyed scribbling notes for fantasy projects she knew she would never write, but which she hoped would give her future biographer something to think about. She was laying a good many little traps for that biographer. Her life had not been dull, but there were things about it that could be improved upon and she was determined to make her biography amusing reading. How many of Georgette Heyer's readers had bothered to read her life? Not many, Moira thought. Now, there had been a truly dull existence. Moira Lockheart's life was to be different! As a true romantic she felt it should give as much pleasure to her readers as her novels. She had not written her autobiography because she did not wish to be found out later in a lie. What assumptions the biographer might make from the evidence she was laying down even now like vintage port was entirely up to him. Moira always thought of her biographer as 'him'. He would be young, regular-featured, muscular, with horn-rimmed spectacles; his pallor denoting years of study in libraries. If you opened his shirt he would be surprisingly hairy, and clad in very tight jeans. His last subject before tackling her would be a biography of Yeats. Moira was rather in love with him.

Her real life had been made up of a series of highly satisfactory unconsummated passions. At least she thought of them as passions. Most of them had been with distinguished homosexuals. When her biographer tackled her life he would find himself revising the received knowledge on a number of well-known men. Just wait, she thought, until he discovered her love affair with Auden. She was, after all, a highly skilled fictional historian. Whenever she thought of Auden, and the bombshell that awaited the public, she shivered with glee.

Whether Auden, in whatever Arcadian grove he was tethered, would be furious at this revision of his sexuality, she preferred not to think. He would probably be sick with rage at being put into bed with her. Not that it was a bed. She had placed them in the passageway between the kitchen

6

and the sitting-room of his apartment in the lower east side of Manhattan. More than once. She had indicated a minimum of four occasions. It was up to the biographer to scour Auden's writing for evidence of their amorous rapture!

She was not without sexual experience. There was one man with whom her relations had been what she thought of as 'thoroughgoing'. She was twenty-nine at the time and had thought that she owed it to her art to do it before she was thirty. She had found the experience uncomfortable and unaesthetic. She could not see where the pleasure lay. She had suffered the same indignity on three further occasions because somewhere she had read that sex improved with practice. Then she retired.

Today she went up in the creaking lift to the fiction stacks hoping to re-immerse herself in the works of Charlotte M. Yonge so as to be in the right frame of mind for the meeting of the Pearls. She thought she would start re-reading the novel from which the society had taken its name: *The Chaplet of Pearls*. Scanning the shelves Moira was disconcerted to find none of Charlotte M. Yonge's novels. This had never happened before. In case they had been placed out of order she spent half an hour looking for them. Was it possible that the London Library had decided to *throw out* Charlotte M. Yonge? Surely not! Katherine and Blanche would never have allowed such a catastrophe to occur. Sinister machinations sometimes took place within the walls of the London Library. There had been an attempt in the seventies to sell the building. Uneasy excitement filled her. Her heart beat heavy in her chest and she sat down on a chair to regain her breath. Breathing slowly, trying to cancel out the fright, she felt death stroke her face. When her body quietened she struggled with difficulty to her feet. Her limbs felt feeble and unwilling to move, and for once she was pleased by the slow creaking descent of the lift.

Recovering in the calm of the green Reading Room Moira noticed a pretty girl at the far end surrounded by familiar-looking volumes. She hesitated. Members did not like being interrupted when they were working, but this was too important. Taboos existed to be broken. Approaching the table where the girl was studying, Moira pulled up a chair and sitting very close to her whispered, 'You like Charlotte M. Yonge, do you?'

Hilary Greep stared at the large smiling old woman who was craning to look at her writing pad and said, 'Somewhat.'

The pretty little thing had a regional accent. More an intonation really, Moira thought. Moira was not very good at placing accents, and had found her lack of an ear a drawback when setting out to write historical novels. Until the nineteenth century most people had regional accents. Later, she had risen above such considerations.

'She *is* a wonderful writer, isn't she? I realise I am interrupting you, but I can't describe how exciting it is to discover such a young *aficionado* of her art. Would you come and have tea with me? You don't know what pleasure it would give me if you would. And who knows, you might discover something to your advantage as well.' Moira beamed at her.

Hilary hesitated. She wanted to work. She was making a list of all the fathers in Charlotte M. Yonge's novels under the headings, Dead, Flawed, and Exemplary, and she had no desire to discuss Yonge's work with some enthusiastic, primitive reader.

'Did you know the Literary Society is to have a lecture on

her in three weeks' time, and I have reason to believe that I am to give it!' Moira whispered persuasively. Although she had not as yet heard from Katherine, she had been in touch with one of the Pearls, Maisy Armstrong, who had mentioned that she was to be asked to give the lecture.

Reluctantly, Hilary tidied her papers, put them in a satchel and followed Moira out of the building.

The café they found to sit in was Italian and not very clean. They decided on coffee as the safest option, agreeing that Italians rarely knew how to make drinkable tea.

'Have you just discovered Charlotte M. Yonge or did you come across her novels when you were a child?' Moira asked when they were settled with their *cappuccinos*.

'I have been investigating nineteenth-century literature and found what I needed in Charlotte M. Yonge.'

'You are studying her?' Moira was relieved. Hilary was no more than a pretty child. 'How nice that universities have at long last caught up with her. Where do you study?'

'London. But I'm not an undergraduate. I'm doing a postgraduate degree and writing a life of Charlotte M. Yonge.'

'How interesting!' Moira no longer felt relieved. 'You probably know that there have been two lives written already and that all her papers were destroyed by her first biographer.'

'Yes, that was one of the attractions,' Hilary said in what Moira thought was a rather enigmatic manner.

'I'm a writer too,' Moira said gaily. 'Let me introduce myself. I'm Moira Lockheart.' She paused expectantly. She was not disappointed.

'Oh I've read lots of your books!' Hilary spoke enthusiastically and was careful not to add that she had read them when she was fourteen. She had once made the mistake of telling an elderly novelist that she had much enjoyed her books as a child. The novelist had replied acidly, 'How nice for you, dear,' and then added, 'They were not intended for children.'

Moira beamed at her and for a moment forgot her dismay in finding that this strange girl of unknown origin was laying claim to her heroine.

Hilary added, 'Do please tell me, is Moira Lockheart your real name? I have often wondered.'

Moira was disconcerted. 'Yes. Absolutely. I was christened Moira Laeticia Lockheart.'

'Moira Laeticia Lockheart,' Hilary repeated. 'I like Laeticia. I think if I had been you I would have called myself Laeticia. Laeticia Greep. No. I think Hilary is better. Hilary Greep.'

Moira felt the conversation slipping away from her. 'Who is Hilary Greep?'

'I'm Hilary Greep.'

'I see.' Moira did not see. 'And is Hilary Greep not your real name?' she asked tentatively.

'Yes,' Hilary said, 'it's very real.'

Moira decided that she had asked a silly question. Who would voluntarily call themselves Hilary Greep? 'Did you know that a group of admirers of Charlotte M. Yonge meets periodically to discuss her work? We call our group The Chaplet of Pearls after her historical novel of that name. We are the pearls in a chaplet crowning the glorious head of Charlotte M. Yonge! It does, I think, define the manner and spirit of our group rather well. It might be of interest to you to know that we have most of the papers that survived Miss Coleridge's frenzy of destruction. Perhaps you would like to attend one of our meetings? I am sure everybody would be very interested in meeting a new biographer of Miss Yonge. Quite a few of us are writers but we have never felt there was enough new material to tackle the subject of her life afresh.'

'My approach is more tangential. It is the gaps in the narrative of her life that I find interesting.'

'How fascinating,' Moira said. 'You must tell us all about it.'

'Why not?' It was unlikely that the group would have anything interesting to add to her thesis but it would be as wrong to overlook an avenue of research as it would be awkward were she to find any evidence around to contradict her theories about Charlotte M. Yonge.

'First, though, you must come to my lecture on the 26th of March at the Literary Society. Do you know about the Literary Society? If not you should join. They have all sorts of functions. After my lecture I will introduce you to the members of our little group. Most of them will be there. We started out with sixteen members, but of course some have drifted away and some have died. So there are not very many of us left now.'

'I would love to attend your lecture,' Hilary said with as much social warmth as she felt was advisable on such short acquaintance. She made a note of the time and place, and avoided Moira's suggestion of picking her up in a taxi and taking her there.

The following day Moira decided she should share the news about this new young biographer who had come into her life and so she rang Katherine. Katherine was out and there was only the answering machine to speak to and Moira was not going to speak to that, so she rang Georgina Matheson instead.

Chapter Two

Georgina Matheson was still in her nightdress and dressing gown when Moira rang at eleven o'clock to tell her about the young girl writing the life of Charlotte M. Yonge. She was of course interested, but could not summon up the excitement Moira seemed to think her news warranted. She had only just replaced the receiver and was sitting at her dressing table peering forward into the glass and painting her face, when Georgio entered her bedroom from his adjoining one.

'You need spectacles, you know,' he said.

'No, I don't.'

'You do. You had better get dressed. Christopher is due in half an hour.'

Christopher was her son.

'He can't be. What time is it?'

'Half-past eleven. He's taking you out to lunch.'

'I don't want to go. We'll eat here.'

'He won't eat here; he says it's not hygienic.'

She sighed. 'We'll see.'

Georgina Matheson hated going out. She had married at the age of twenty-six, and a week after returning from the honeymoon had taken to her bed and not risen from it until six years and three children later when her husband left her. Having then got used to the indoors she still preferred it to the noise, fluctuations in temperature and bustle of the outside world. Occasionally she went abroad for a month or so and stayed with friends in their villa in Greece. It was on one of these occasions, some twenty years previously, that she met Georgio and brought him home with her. On the whole the arrangement had worked well for both of them. They lived in the house in Belgravia she had been brought to as a bride, which would have been very grand if it had not been so dilapidated. It was about this house that Christopher wished to talk to her, if possible without Georgio being present. Although his mother had always lived in the house, it actually belonged to his father, who had left her there even after the children had grown up because he was unable to face the hullabaloo of trying to dislodge her. Now his father was dead and Christopher had inherited it. It was a question less of avarice than possession. The house was his and he could not watch it disintegrate into a ruin. His mother must be moved or made to change her habits. He was not looking forward to their lunch.

The house reeked of dry rot. Though visitors looked nervously around for a gas leak Georgina Matheson had lived with the stench too long to notice it. Georgio suspected old age had affected her sense of smell. Certainly her eyesight was not what it was. A few weeks ago he had taken a large Imari pot from the top of the bookcase in the drawing-room and sold it to a dealer on Kensington Church Street without her noticing its absence. When he had done that a year ago she had shrieked at him, hit him with her stick, and demanded it back. But if Georgina's sense of smell had gone age had not affected her sense of taste. At Christmas he had tried passing

13

off his gift of lump-fish roe as caviare but she had known at once. She had thought that quite funny.

When Christopher arrived, his mother was not yet dressed and so Georgio entertained him. Together they stood in the immense drawing-room, originally designed as a ballroom, where in Christopher's youth dances had often taken place. Now a billiard table took up one end, the furniture and fireplace the other. There was little harmony. In his mind's eye Christopher could not help seeing it divided. Perhaps one half a library and the other a sitting-room. Would dividing the windows be a problem?

Georgio offered him a glass of Cyprus sherry, a vile drink to which Georgina was addicted. He had his own supply of whisky which Georgina loathed and for which she refused to pay. Georgio did not choose to offer this to Christopher, although he sometimes offered it to Christopher's son Robert and daughter Robina. But then, in a way, they helped pay for it since he supplemented his lack of sufficient income by supplying his youthful acquaintances with cocaine, marijuana and assorted pills. This had started innocently. He and Georgina had always enjoyed the odd snort, roll-up and tablet. In consequence, it had not taken Georgina's teenage grandchildren long to discover that their grandmother's house was rather more entertaining than their parents'. As they entered their twenties they introduced their friends to Georgio and before he clearly understood what was happening his allowance from Georgina had become inflation-proof. She had become increasingly mean in old age and Georgio did, after all, have to get by somehow.

Conversation was awkward – Christopher did not like Georgio much; he suspected that he supplied his children with drugs. Considering their respective relationships to Georgina, they were too close in age to be comfortable together. Christopher was fifty-six and Georgio sixty-four. When Georgina entered the room they were talking with seeming friendliness about Christopher's wish to grow thousands of conifers on his estate in Argyll.

At eighty-three, Georgina had shrunk and swollen. Her once elegant and colourful clothes now looked dishevelled, and her crumpled face, although carefully made-up, was an over-bright appendage to the general jumble of clothing. She walked with a stick as she suffered from bad circulation of the legs.

'Hello, darling.' She presented a cheek to Christopher who kissed it. Georgio gave her a glass of sherry.

'We had better go. I have booked a table for one o'clock,' Christopher said.

'Can't we stay here? I don't as a general rule eat lunch.'

'But I do; and I'm hungry.' Christopher was firm.

'I'm sure we could give you a sandwich or something.' Georgina looked enquiringly at Georgio.

Georgio had mercy on Christopher. He did not dislike him. 'There is absolutely nothing here. Percy is doing the shopping on her way in this afternoon.' Percy was the cleaner who also did for Katherine.

'Oh dear! Well, I must drink my sherry first.' She took tiny sips.

Christopher sat forward in his chair showing irritable tension in his frame. 'I have to be back at the office by half-past two.'

'Back to the bank.' Georgio laughed. He found any mention of banks irresistibly funny.

Christopher and Georgina ignored him.

At one o'clock Georgina's glass was empty. Christopher

knew that his suppressed irritation did not augur well for the conversation ahead. Georgio saw them out. He then went to the kitchen and made himself a mayonnaise, Gruyère and tongue sandwich, put it on a tray with a glass of milk and returned to the drawing-room.

In the dark surroundings of a Chinese restaurant in Beauchamp Place, Georgina made the first move. 'Before I married your father, I spent four months in China,' she began.

Christopher interrupted. He had heard the story before. 'I want to talk about the house.'

'Oh!'

'It really does need work done on it.'

'I can't afford it.'

'But I can.'

Georgina was no fool. 'It will see me out.'

'It won't, you know.'

'I don't want a lot of workmen in, banging around.'

'I know, I've thought of that.' He shovelled a monosodium glutamate mess into his mouth without pleasure. 'I was thinking that perhaps you would be more comfortable, now that your legs aren't so good, in a nice flat with a lift and porterage.'

'I don't see that I would. What would I need with a lift? I don't go out except once or twice a year to attend The Chaplet of Pearls.'

'You go out a lot more than that.'

'I don't.'

'You do.'

'You don't know what I do,' she said crossly, and then, quickly, 'and that is not a reproach.'

'You're getting on, Mummy,' he said pleadingly.

'I manage quite well and Georgio is young. And what about Georgio? What were you proposing to do with Georgio? Boot him out?'

'No, of course not. He would go with you.'

'It would not suit.'

'Why not?'

'We need a lot of room around us. He likes to get away, be on a separate floor to work, with a staircase between him and me.'

'What work?' Christopher asked, now cross.

'He has an office and does what men usually do in them. I have never found it necessary to enquire further.'

He tried again. 'Mummy, I'm sorry, but I have to push you on this. The house is falling down. It's mine. I am not trying to push you out. I'll consider any suggestions you have so long as the work gets done. My guess is that the work will take three or four months and I do think you and Georgio would be more comfortable out of the house while it is going on.'

'Once the work was done, I would return?'

'You would return.'

'It's well known that old people die or go gaga when they are made to leave their homes. I expect you are hoping that will happen to me. Then you can sell it or move in.'

'I cannot imagine killing you off so easily.'

'I'll think about it,' she said, not meaning to do any such thing.

Christopher suspected she intended to give the conversation no more thought. The lunch was merely the opening shot across her bow. They talked of other things: about his wife Jane, about his son Robert's beautiful black girlfriend and about how well Robina was doing at Broadlands, the drug clinic. 'She's looking wonderful,' Christopher told her.

'She's filled out a little and seems right on top of things. The only thing is she has formed a romantic attachment to one of the other inmates, who's converted her to vegetarianism, which is a bit of a bore. But we're relieved to see her looking so well.'

Robina was supposed to be Georgina's favourite grandchild as she had insisted that she should be named after one of her favourite children, the conscientious, big-hearted Robina in *The Pillars of the House*, by her favourite writer Charlotte M. Yonge. Of all Charlotte M. Yonge's novels, read and re-read many times, it was *The Pillars of the House* Georgina loved best. Alas, as it turned out Robina was not one of her favourite grandchildren. As a child she had been quarrelsome, noisy, and prone to breaking things, while now she was given to assaulting her boyfriends and attempting suicide. Georgina also found her gluttony for drugs, drink, and egg mayonnaise sandwiches tedious. She did, however, play along with Jane and Christopher's belief in her special interest in Robina, who, of course, sensed the lie. By way of revenge, Robina was in the habit of staging a good many of her dramas in Georgina's house.

'It is because we have not been at war for such a long time,' Georgina said. 'There is nothing like shortages to make people like meat. Look at Eastern Europe. They are always complaining that they haven't enough of the stuff.'

'How about the Indians? They are perfectly happy with their hot vegetables.'

'Yes, of course, there are always the Indians and there always will be.' Georgina moved on to another tack. 'Vegetarianism wasn't a problem for the Victorians. I can remember no mention of it in Dickens and Thackeray and it is certainly never raised as an issue in Charlotte M. Yonge. I wonder if there is enough there to write a paper on the lack of vegetarian sensibility in the Victorian novel with particular reference to Charlotte M. Yonge? It is becoming very difficult to find new topics to talk about at our meetings. What do you think?'

'A bit thin.'

'Perhaps,' Georgina said. 'Perhaps I could tie it up with the Church of England. Vegetarianism isn't really a very Church of England thing, is it? Anti-magnetic. I think you might possibly argue that it is a side-effect of agnosticism – like dieting and the cult of youth.' She rummaged in her bag for the notebook she always carried to jot down interesting things. 'I shall ring Katherine. She is always very severe on woolly ideas such as mine,' she said cheerfully.

Katherine Sackville was in the kitchen wearing rubber gloves and a surgical mask when Georgina rang. She was doing one of the tasks of the day she most loathed, feeding Mozart, Brahms, M. Yonge, Rossetti and Browning their Pedigree Chum. Her five expectant Pekinese looked up at her, tails waving, as she doled the stuff out into five bowls. She hated the smell, its consistency and the plopping noise it made as it went into the bowls. It put her off eating. She heard Georgina's voice coming from the sitting-room, quacking on the answering machine, but made no attempt to lift the receiver of the telephone beside her on the kitchen counter. She did not believe in interrupting the tasks of the day, particularly if they were unpleasant. She still sometimes missed her husband, Kenneth, horribly. He had always fed the dogs. They had no children; for both had been too busy, and Katherine in particular saw little pleasure in the prospect of kissing dirty faces, wiping noses, having

19

sticky fingers on the furniture and perpetual mess. She had been the only child of elderly parents and had found being grown-up a good deal more comfortable than childhood. As headmistress of Merton School she could only commiserate with the children on their condition of immature servitude, and had seen her role as that of hastening forward as fast as possible the desirable state of adulthood for her girls.

The first change she had made in the school was to cancel all cookery and sewing classes. She could not boil an egg herself and had often thought about how many thousands of hours she had saved for her work simply by failing to master the unnatural art of stirring things together. Now that her husband was dead she went less often to restaurants and instead survived on a diet of apples, bananas and peanut-butter sandwiches. When the need for something different overwhelmed her she would go to a mediocre Italian restaurant three minutes' walk away in Notting Hill Gate, and unselfconsciously read a book as she devoured Wiener schnitzel and chips. Breakfast she had mastered at Girton. She made an excellent cup of strong coffee and drank it with hot milk accompanied by toast and Tiptree Little Scarlet Strawberry Jam.

Although Katherine had never particularly liked children she had always enjoyed reading about them. Of course she recognised that fictional children were an edited version of the real thing. This was part of the pleasure of the novels of Charlotte M. Yonge. In their pages, Katherine could wax indignant at childhood injustices, and empathise with their troubles – without having to cope with the trite reality of the real thing. It was, in fact, because of this sanitised interest in children that she had come to devour the novels of Charlotte M. Yonge, taken one by one from a set in her mother's bedroom. And it was this that led her, with Blanche Chambers, a fellow enthusiast whom she had come upon at a party forty years ago, to form The Chaplet of Pearls.

For several years, she had taken a sixth-form class in literature at Merton and quite enjoyed the experience. After teaching at Birkbeck College during the turbulent sixties she had been pleased to escape into the calmer climes of producing confident and motivated young women. Though she knew few of their names, her pupils liked her. They considered her glamorous. This was partly style. She had always dressed elegantly if somewhat old-fashionedly and she had particularly good legs. These gave her a youthful air. To this day she had firm, high-coloured skin. She was quite vain and liked the fact that she was wearing rather better than most of her friends and contemporaries.

With the odorous business of feeding her dogs now over, Katherine stripped off the rubber gloves and went into the sitting-room to listen to Georgina's message. More incoherent than usual, she thought, as 'vegetarianism', 'Charlotte M. Yonge' and 'the Church of England' tumbled from the speaker. She quickly wrote a card saying 'Charlotte M. Yonge and the Church of England: yes. Vegetarianism and Charlotte M. Yonge: no. The Church of England and vegetarianism: no,' and signed it 'K.S.' For good measure she also wrote a letter to Portia.

My dearest Portia,

The next meeting of The Chaplet of Pearls is upon us. I do hope you intend to come up from Somerset for it as I would not wish you to miss my lecture on Plumbing in Rural England Between 1848 and 1870 with Reference

21

to the Works of Charlotte M. Yonge. You are, after all, the only member who might be called a landowner. If only you were a man you could be dignified with the title of Squire. But then if you were a man, I would probably have married you and taken you away from all that. I would love to give you a bed for the night. Do come, we will have such fun. I will take you out to dinner and you can go shopping and get one of those impossibly dowdy tweed skirts you like to wear. If you could drag yourself away for even longer Moira is to give a lecture at the Literary Society on Yonge. Who knows, maybe it will lead to a renaissance of interest in her works!

Love, Katherine
P.S. I seal the envelope with the blackened paw of M. Yonge!

She did, too, and it was quite a struggle to make M. Yonge keep still long enough to press her paw in the black ink and press it down on the envelope. She did not enquire about Portia's husband, Archie, as she preferred not to know.

Slipping into enormous black galoshes (she was very proud of them as they were difficult to come by and had lasted her since the sixties), and putting on an ancient but stylish raincoat, she wound a strongly patterned blue-and-yellow scarf around her neck, wondering whether she should walk the dogs in St James's Park, before visiting the London Library to pick up books. It would mean ordering a minicab. It was years since she had driven. She had given up as soon as she had felt rich enough to take taxis everywhere. At Merton, the school had paid for her regular minicab; at home Kenneth drove. Now, the problem was the pekes. She always left them tied to the railings near the entrance to the Library but the Pekinese seemed bent on attracting the attention of any passing dog thief by barking incessantly until she reappeared.

So she hesitated. She badly needed to find out if Mark Girouard covered sanitation in *The Victorian Country House*, for her lecture on the 30th, since she had been unable to find her own copy, a first edition. She never lent books and so feared it had been pinched. Katherine invariably thought that things she could not find had been stolen but never mentioned the possibility as she suspected it might be a sign of incipient madness in herself. This time, though, she was sure it had been stolen by Teddy Linklater. He was famously poor and always scrounging for a free meal. Also, he always carried a large, battered briefcase full of his unpublished poems. It would be quite easy to slip the odd book into it. She must be careful not to leave him alone in her drawing-room in future.

Katherine decided she *would* go to the London Library. The next ten minutes were an uncomfortable reminder of the sheer awfulness entailed in being alive. Her five dogs had to be attached to five leads. Having done this she realised that she must collect the books to return to the Library. That meant letting go of the dogs. They scattered in the delight of naughtiness. Then she dialled her local minicab company. At last, more than usually exhausted, she set out for St James's Park.

Portia Sheldon was in the garden. With a bitter east wind whistling into her left ear, she could feel the beginning of earache developing. She was turning large clods of heavy clay with a big fork in the border next to the house containing the irises and herb garden. The garden boy Terry, a forty-seven-year-old man whom she got cheaply from the local hostel for the subnormal, had flu so she was finishing off the border for him. Otherwise her chief gardener, old Mr Baxter, would use his absence to complain that the garden was understaffed. What's more, there was no denying that it *was* understaffed. She knew she should let some of it go to sheep, but she loved it. It was laid out, terraced, stepped, balustraded and ornamented with urns and a summer house by Lutyens. Her mother had added a beech avenue now overtaken by rhododendrons, and her son had put in a trout pool with a stone seat and statue.

Hearing the sound of a far-off bell, she allowed her fork to fall and rose with some difficulty to her feet. Walking through the french windows in the dining-room she was conscious of the thick, damp mud clinging to her Wellington boots and tried tiptoeing through the hall hoping that the mud would not become dislodged. She opened the front door to a man in a beige mac who was carrying a small suitcase and who looked like a clerk. Before either of them were able to speak, her daughter came thumping down the bare wooden staircase.

'Don't worry, Mummy darling,' she cried. 'He's for me. He's a water-diviner.'

'But we've plenty of water here and we are practically surrounded by sea.'

'Don't worry, Mummy, I'll explain later.'

'Where are you taking him?' Portia was beginning to feel cross. She wished Anna would not order up water-diviners – or photographers, dress designers, festival organisers, poets or sculptors who wished to tie

24

bits of rubbish to the branches of trees in the meadow
or . . .

'He's going to divine water in the meadow.'

'That won't be difficult.'

A stream ran through the meadow which rolled down to
cliffs edging the sea.

'Not that bit of meadow. He's going to look for deep
underground water. We'll be back in a couple of hours and
I'll tell you all about it.'

Turning disconsolately towards the dining-room, the
french windows and the east wind again, Portia noticed
that the postman had already been. He always left the post
on the hall table. Because there was very little to steal at
Sheldon Hall the front door was rarely locked except at
night. Portia rifled through the letters. There were bills, a
subscription demand from *Farmers Weekly*, an illiterate card
from someone in the village, and a letter from Katherine. She
sat down in the hall, pleased. How nice of Katherine to write.
What a pity she would never come to stay.

Katherine had not been to Sheldon Hall for forty-five
years. After two shatteringly uncomfortable visits she had
decided that she hated the countryside in general and the
English country house in particular and that she would never
stir from London unless it was to go to a major European
capital. She was right not to have relented; Sheldon Hall
had not altered since her last visit. It was a large, rambling
seventeenth-century house whose Victorian additions had
failed to add to its comfort. Portia's family had lived there in
one form or another since it was built, and were inured to its
plentiful discomforts. Of the three sitting-rooms, none could
realistically be described as a drawing-room. One (known
as the music room because it contained a piano) was long,

25

narrow and darkly panelled. In winter it suffered from an icy draught because its door needed to be kept ajar to stop the fire smoking. Here the family and their friends would sing madrigals and sea shanties. The Sheldons were a musical family. Portia played the cello, Anna the flute, and both Mary and Eliza the violin. Harry, still unmarried and the heir to everything, played the piano. Born long after they thought it possible, he was their delight. In fact all the Sheldons played the piano but since Harry had no other instrument the piano was thought of as his. In the past Archie, their father, had also sung most melodiously. He had changed his name from Roberts to Sheldon when he married Portia. His life had been spent hunting, re-designing the garden, and managing the estate. He could still, when called upon for some harmonising, hum a bit. He had met Portia, a war widow, in 1950 when they were both singing in a Christmas production of *The Messiah* in Taunton. Portia had mistaken the narcissistic pleasure they both felt when singing in harmony for religious exultation. He had been a career officer in the army but when they became engaged had resigned his commission, moved his horses to Sheldon Hall and taken over the running of the estate, including the village of Clompton. Of the three daughters, Eliza and Mary were married with children and living in the north of England.

Another sitting-room on the first floor was so small that more than three people made it feel crowded. The furniture was arranged in such a way that it necessitated the head being turned sideways in order to address anyone, or as Katherine pointed out, 'for three Sheldons to sit adjacent to each other with eyes fixed sideways in as comfortable a position as they knew how'. The third sitting-room was decorated with a brightly coloured French baroque wallpaper depicting gods and goddesses out hunting. This was officially known as the sunken drawing-room but rarely used. Its entrance was eight feet above the floor. Guests, feeling as though they were immersing themselves in a fish tank, descended down a stair into the room.

There were other discomforts to the house. Although a sufficient sprinkling of Victorian cast-iron radiators was dotted about, it made little impression on the cold. Katherine was fond of describing how, when in bed in Sheldon Hall with the regulation three blankets and an eiderdown, cold air radiated out through the soft flesh of the stomach as the victim breathed in.

Summers of course were different. Discomfort fell away. Guests would be entertained out of doors with long walks, painful swimming among rocky coves, rough, frightening bare-back riding on wildly undisciplined horses whose eyes rolled in their sockets, delicious picnics, visits to picturesque pubs and for those so inclined, expeditions to antique and second-hand bookshops. For the most part Sheldon was much loved by its visitors: the wild and beautiful landscape reflected the inner rhythm of the household. When young, Portia's children would hold court with their friends in separate house parties, the members of one gang greeting those of another amiably as they passed each other coming and going. The system appeared to operate spontaneously. There was little domestic 'help' and what there was was cheeky and under-age. In its place Portia relied on her own inner steel, which beneath her warm, soft manner was considerable, and which would show itself in sharp reminders to her daughters to clear up the kitchen, peel the potatoes or feed the chickens. Portia usually retired at ten o'clock and rose at six-thirty, but whatever hour the household might retire to bed one of her children if at home would accompany her to Sunday morning service at the village church at 8 a.m. Her tentatively expressed suggestions disguised an iron will.

Those not of Katherine's urban persuasion loved the place. Writers went down to write. Those with broken romances went there to breathe fresh air, and go for long walks with Portia. Those recuperating from illness would wander in the garden and read in the summer house.

Not all the rooms were uncomfortable. The large kitchen with its Aga was warm and inviting and the dining-room was a well-proportioned square room with french windows leading out on to a pretty terrace. Portia was a good, old-fashioned cook who made her own bread and cakes but hated waste. Remembering the war, she had been known to offer the remains on a guest's plate to the assembled company.

Her first feeling on reading Katherine's letter was to think that she could not possibly go up to London for the meeting. Although she had known about it for some months and (unusually for her) written it into her diary, she had not seriously considered going. She considered the date of the meeting . . . There was Archie to think about, Archie who, she suddenly remembered, she had left in the summer house looking at a picture book as she worked in the flower border. He would probably have wandered off by now.

She looked out of the window. There was no sign of him. Getting up she went out and checked the summer house. It was empty; only the book remained. She looked down across the meadows in the direction of the sea. The day was darkening. In the distance she could see the water-diviner and her daughter who was gesticulating some little way away from him. He was standing still. Really Anna *was* irritating and completely unsuitably dressed for the weather.

She was wearing a long-sleeved T-shirt, a leather jerkin, an ankle-length cotton skirt, and was bare-legged with dirty gym shoes. Her curly brown hair was blowing wildly. She was forty-two years old, childless, and recently divorced. The eyes of a startled horse looked out of her pretty, neat-featured face. Portia worried about her.

Turning indoors Portia decided that Archie was bound to bump into someone – he always did – and be returned. As she took off her boots and washed her hands she wondered if it would be possible to take off for a couple of days. It would mean finding someone to look after Archie. Anna, even if she were still here, was not to be trusted. She would take him for a ride and accidentally allow him to drop over the cliff, or they would go for an impossible walk and she would be unable to get him back. Portia had a vision of Archie slowly toppling off Fallada, one of the half-wild, seldom ridden horses, and falling head first slowly, slowly down into the sea. She sighed and mentally crossed herself. She could see if Mrs Willis would come up from the village. It would be nice to have a cosy evening with Katherine full of astringent chat, eat in a good restaurant, perhaps buy a pair of shoes, see some exhibitions and go to the saddler's in South Audley Street. If very tempted she might buy some modern riding helmets for her grandchildren for when they came to stay. The old ones, so much more becoming, were now frowned upon as unsafe. She would put off writing to Katherine until she had time to think about it.

Chapter Three

The Literary Society was located in Earls Court Square on two floors of a large-pillared house. In a room off the white-panelled lecture hall the committee fortified Moira with a large gin and tonic. Moira hardly needed it; she quite enjoyed giving lectures.

She faced the audience from behind a lectern. Not a very large audience, she thought, perhaps twenty-five. There was Katherine sitting next to Maisy in her wheelchair. Neither of the Annabels nor Portia had made the meeting. Good, there was Georgina with Grace. Not a bad turn-out really. She scanned the audience looking for the pretty face of Hilary Greep. Surely she would not miss it?

'Good evening,' she began. 'I wish to say, first, how honoured I am to be asked to give this address on the Victorian writer and novelist Charlotte M. Yonge. And perhaps before launching forth I should first explain why I am being so honoured. My name is Moira Lockheart and I belong to a small group of Miss Yonge's admirers who meet once or twice a year to discuss her work. It was I who suggested calling our group The Chaplet of Pearls after her historical novel of that name. It does, I think, define the manner and spirit of our group rather well. The Chaplet of Pearls was formed in 1955 when Blanche Chambers, a research scientist then working at Portman Research Laboratory, met Lady Sackville, then headmistress of Merton School for Girls, at a party and discovered their mutual enthusiasm for the works of Charlotte M. Yonge. Blanche Chambers was our first Chairman but sadly is not here this evening as she had a stroke at Christmas. Blanche came to be an admirer of Charlotte M. Yonge because of her work. She claimed that if you spent all your time cutting up, poisoning, gassing and dissecting animals in a laboratory you were likely to gain a religious perspective on life. This led her, perfectly naturally, to Charlotte M. Yonge.'

The logic was not entirely clear to everyone present, but one or two nodded politely.

'I, on the other hand, discovered her historical novels for children when I was six, and so naturally became devoted to her adult historical novels. They in their turn led to my interest in medieval history. The rest, it could be said, is my history.' She paused and smiled.

The audience laughed in acknowledgement of her pun. She did not need to explain that she was a popular writer of historical novels.

'Others, I am very well aware, are more particularly struck by her family sagas and novels for young ladies. Because of this, I am concentrating on this aspect of her work in my talk.' She looked up to show that she had finished her preamble and saw Hilary Greep tiptoe in and sit at the back of the room.

'In *The Heir of Redclyffe*, the fourth and most popular of all Charlotte M. Yonge's novels,' she began, 'the young hero Sir Guy Morville refuses to take his horse to Oxford in case the town should corrupt the morals of his groom. This example of excessive high-mindedness embodies both the pleasure and perhaps – considering her now reduced status in the consciousness of the public – the drawback of reading the novels of the spinster author, Charlotte M. Yonge. In its time such high-mindedness was accepted by the public without the least difficulty. When Guy died, Dante Gabriel Rossetti wept, and William Morris, Tennyson and Charles Kingsley were deeply affected. Hundreds of soldiers carried the book to the Crimean War.

'Charlotte M. Yonge was the most popular novelist of her day. She wrote around one hundred and sixty books during her long life, some of them of an exclusively edifying nature, but all her novels seem to hook readers who have the luck to come upon them. Some of us, in this room, have had that luck.' She looked up and eyed her audience.

'The pleasures of a Charlotte M. Yonge novel are hard to pin down. She does not write elegant prose. Sometimes quite the contrary. The agonies her characters go through to become good people have the reader fighting a rear-guard action against the severity of the moral strictures that she lays upon them. Their smallest fault can cause sweat, tears, prayers, illness and death. It is in this emotionally violent inner struggle over apparently small things that the reader finds her satisfaction. Charlotte M. Yonge has a brilliant facility for characterising the young. In the novels for adults they are real people who, against the reader's wishes, grow up, change and become good. Some, whose failings in character have been signalled since childhood, fall by the wayside. Their fate is dire – almost as dire are those who triumph and become good. One such favourite is Ethel in *The Daisy Chain*. Ethel chooses to deny her own chances of fulfilment to dedicate her life to her father. The novel ends with this reflection on her future: "Home! but her eyes had been opened to see that earthly homes may not endure, nor fill the heart. Her dear father might, indeed, claim her full-hearted devotion, but, to him she was one of many . . . and she had begun to understand that the unmarried woman must not seek undivided return of affection, and must not set her love, with exclusive eagerness, on aught below, but must be ready to cease in turn to be the first with any."

'Nobody could accuse Charlotte M. Yonge of being a romantic writer! The dismay any modern reader must feel on Ethel's behalf is profound. Is it for this that we have suffered with her in her battle with inky fingers and careless dress, her heroic struggle to keep up with her brother in her Greek studies? Was it for this that we entered into her enthusiasm for church building and helping the rural poor? There is a terrible realism in Ethel's reflection on her future. Even if *she* does not feel that her fate is an unhappy one, the reader is filled with dismay that all that promise and delicacy of mind should be sacrificed. To us her readiness "to cease in turn to be the first with any" seems tragic.

'Usually, though, marriage to a good man is the plateau on which her beloved and beleaguered heroines eventually land. Although there is much blessing in this fate, Miss Yonge does not believe in bliss. The engagement is usually painfully arrived at, and long in duration. As often as not, by the time the marriage takes place, the bridegroom has fallen into poor health. Charlotte M. Yonge's heroines are not, however, mere ciphers of goodness. They have faults and can seriously misjudge the management of others with culpable results.

'What engaged Charlotte M. Yonge was religion and duty. Her ideas of pleasure and relaxation are to sing in the choir, to

33

be confirmed, or to witness a wonderful church service. Shame comes from the dereliction of duty, from the telling of a single untruth, or, in the case of men and boys, rejection of religion or the influence of rough friends. The last mentioned of these might gamble or drink, but real depravity rarely arises. (I am aware that those of you here familiar with her novels will point to the heroine's father in *Nutty's Father* and I suppose others will argue that the charming and dissolute Edgar in *The Pillars of the House* is a bad'un.) But the energy of feeling that goes into even the smallest peccadilloes of her good characters is the real, absorbing drama of her fiction. In *The Pillars of the House*, twelve orphaned children of a very poor but aristocratic clergyman are kept together by the sixteen-year-old eldest son, Felix, and his fifteen-year-old sister, Wilmet. Felix sacrifices both university and his natural station in life as a gentleman (this in Charlotte M. Yonge's terms is serious stuff) to the family's need by apprenticing himself to a printer. Wilmet sacrifices her youth by taking on all the duties of a housewife and teaching at a local primary school. Had Dickens portrayed Wilmet, she would have been a soft, sweet, most womanly young thing with a bunch of keys, dispensing kindness and wisdom. Charlotte M. Yonge has a far more realistic grasp of psychology than this. Deprived of youth but not goodness, Wilmet grows impatient and often intolerant of the foibles of her younger siblings. Worse, she sees only the material imperatives before her, unable to grasp that a small change in her list of priorities might result in an infinite blessing to one of them.

'Not all her contemporary novels are family chronicles like *The Daisy Chain* or *The Pillars of the House*. Some, like *Heartsease* and *The Young Stepmother*, deal specifically with marriage. These novels open with young brides having to tackle formidable tasks unaided by their husbands, whom Charlotte M. Yonge depicts as weak, wayward, lazy and oppressive. Despite Miss Yonge's view that men were ordained by God to be women's superiors, they are only saved to take their places as worthy heads of households through the steely integrity of their women.

'There have been only two biographies of Charlotte M. Yonge. The first and worst is an unbelievably turgid effort by a relative of hers called Christabel Coleridge who destroyed all Miss Yonge's papers when she had finished. The second biography, subtitled *The Story of an Uneventful Life*, is by Georgina Battiscombe. Although excellent, Battiscombe's biography is extremely short. It was published during the war on very cheap paper and went into five imprints in the course of sixteen months.

'Charlotte M. Yonge's life *was* uneventful. She was born in 1823. Her father was a small landowner and they lived in the Hampshire village of Otterbourne where William Yonge built the church. His best friend was John Keble, one of the founding members of the Oxford Movement and Vicar of the neighbouring village of Hursley. Miss Yonge was therefore brought up on Tractarian principles. John Keble prepared her for confirmation at fifteen and it was at this point that religion became the focal point of her life. The other major influence in her life was her father, who was both her teacher and mentor well into adulthood. They were very close. In fact, it could be said that she only ceased to be his pupil on his death, when she was thirty-nine. Fathers, and the duty owed to them, loom large in her fiction. They come before the claims of lovers and all self-will is subdued to their wishes. Only God's law can wrest initiative from them. When the heroine is married, the cloak of her father's august supremacy is thrown upon the shoulders of the husband, however inadequate he may be to wear it. From this you will realise that Charlotte M. Yonge is no feminist.' She looked up in order to emphasise the point. 'When in old age her help was solicited by those wishing to start a college for women, she replied, "I am obliged to you for your letter respecting the proposed College for Ladies, but as I have decided objections to bringing large masses of girls together and think that home education under the inspection and encouragement of sensible fathers, or voluntarily continued by the girls themselves, is far more valuable both intellectually and morally than any external education . . . I am afraid I cannot assist you." She then goes on, "I feel with much regret that female education is deficient, but I think the way to meet the evil is by rousing parents to lead their daughters to read, think, and converse. All the most superior women I have known have been thus formed, by *home* influence, and I think that girls in large numbers always hurt one another in manner and tone if in nothing else. Superior women will teach themselves, and inferior women will never learn more than enough for home life."

'If Charlotte M. Yonge had gone to school she might well not have developed into the scholarly woman she became. Perhaps her enthusiasm for history, the classics and foreign languages would have been blunted, but on the other hand she might have had an easier, more sociable time in later life. She was a highly strung, excitable, clumsy child who suffered from acute shyness. She gives an endearing portrait of herself at that time in the form of the passionate, wilful, untidy, and misunderstood heroine of one of her best and shortest novels, *Countess Kate*.' Here Moira looked up from her paper. 'If anyone should come across a copy of it, could they let me know as I do not have it and badly want one.

'Although educated at home she was not entirely solitary. Her father's relations had many progeny. In one family alone there were ten children. Charlotte Yonge's yearly visits to these families were the highlight of her childhood and from them she learned about the children who people her novels. What's more, a brother was born when she was seven, by which time, extraordinarily, she was teaching Sunday school. Her first novel *Abbey Church*, published when she was twenty, very nearly did not come out. Her grandmother on her mother's side, with whom they all lived, felt strongly that it was not ladylike to write for money. In the end Charlotte Yonge and her family assuaged their collective conscience by deciding that it would be all right as long as any money she earned went to charity. From then onwards, every evening Charlotte read what she had written that day to her father, who criticised and amended it. It would be wrong to psychoanalyse Miss Yonge from beyond the grave, but let me just observe that in her fiction it is surprising how often her characters are liberated from parental authority by being orphaned or, alternatively, sacrifice a good part of their lives at the behest of quite dreadful fathers.

'In 1851 she started a periodical called the *Monthly Packet* which she edited for forty years until 1890. It was dedicated to informing young women of the principles of Tractarianism. Many of her novels were serialised in it. Her father's death in 1854 devastated her. Ever after, she was enveloped in a certain melancholy. She moved out of her childhood home with her mother to a smaller house, and Keble took on the role of mentor. Now, as her mother became senile, she did not enjoy nursing her. Cut off by her shyness from all but her closest friends, her late novels are not as good as those of her early or middle period. Possibly this is because as she became old she finally lost sympathy with the young. Like Queen Victoria, she died much mourned in 1901 and perhaps, like her, she epitomises much that the nineteenth century stood for.

'Charlotte M. Yonge's imagination never grew up (in old age it merely withered) and her thinking never progressed beyond that of a very precocious, very clever teenager. Those precepts that she had accepted at fifteen never altered or wavered for the rest of her life. In childhood her nervous and excitable imagination became encumbered by a solemn respect for authority. This, coupled with crippling shyness, meant that she never attempted to break free from the bonds of familial duty. Those of her characters who attempt to do so come to sticky ends. She was not, however, conspicuously unhappy. There is no evidence that she ever fell in love. God, her father and John Keble were enough for her emotional needs.' Moira folded her lecture and looked expectantly at her audience. They clapped vigorously.

'Any questions?' Moira asked.

A man put up his hand.

'Yes?'

'How do we get hold of these books?'

'You can find them in second-hand book shops and sometimes in catalogues.'

'I badly want *The Armourer's Prentices*. Would anyone here have a second copy?' a cheerful woman in the front row enquired.

Moira guiltily reflected that she had two copies of *The Armourer's Prentices*. It was her favourite of the historical novels for children. Set in the reign of Henry VIII, it told the story of two orphaned boys who are forced to leave home and make their way in London, after their elder brother marries.

She decided to keep quiet. One was part of a uniform edition, but the other had a pretty embossed picture on the cover.

Another hand was raised. 'I think your lecture was excellent but I have one small quibble,' said an elderly woman in the third row. 'You do rather dismiss Miss Yonge's non-fiction as being of "an exclusively edifying nature". Some of us here, not least myself, are particularly interested in her religious thoughts and precepts for a good life, and I would have thought that her pamphlet *Religious Education of the Wealthier Classes* and her book *Womankind* are worthy of mention. Both exemplify that side of her rather well.'

Rival organisation, Moira thought. 'This was really an introductory talk explaining to those who have never read her why they might like to do so. Any other questions?'

Another hand went up. 'Miss Yonge's characters often fall ill and they hardly ever fully recover. I would be very interested to know if her descriptions of illnesses are accurate?'

Another *aficionado*, thought Moira. 'My feeling is that Charlotte M. Yonge is reflecting a widespread reaction the Victorians felt when a friend or member of the family had so much as a cold. We forget how much our lives have been transformed by antibiotics and pain killers.'

There was a pause, and the Chairman of the Literary Society came forward from a seat in the front row.

'Well, all that is left is to say how grateful we are to Moira Lockheart for telling us about Charlotte M. Yonge. I, for one, cannot wait to read some of her novels and I am sure there are many in the audience who feel the same. Thank you.'

The audience clapped.

Moira, her thoughts on Hilary Greep, pushed forward through the audience, not stopping for those who wished to congratulate her. 'Hilary!' she said gladly, clasping her hand between both of hers. 'Let me introduce you to some of the Pearls.'

Hilary, who had been edging along the side of the room for the exit, was reluctantly led between groups of people to where Katherine was talking to Maisy Armstrong in her wheelchair.

'Maisy, Katherine, let me introduce Hilary Greep who is writing a biography of our heroine!'

They shook hands. 'Moira told us about you. It is very interesting to meet you. Not many of your age group are interested in Charlotte M. Yonge's novels,' Maisy said. Maisy was a big-boned woman of eighty, with a beaky nose powdered whitely and swathed in dusty-looking black clothes. She had a formidable presence. Five years back her rheumatoid arthritis had become so crippling that she was now unable to walk. It was twenty years since she had written a biography and fifteen years since her husband David had died. The two of them had often tackled married couples. David had written the husband's life while Maisy had done the wife's. The publishers had promoted them in tandem and this had helped with sales. Their marriage had been an enjoyable battleground as they fought over the debris of the marriages of the long dead. Together they had done the Brownings, the Marlboroughs, the Byrons and the Carlyles. Now her daughter Laura looked after her.

'Yes,' Hilary said.

'You must come to our next meeting of the Pearls on the 30th,' Maisy said looking at Katherine. 'Katherine is to give a talk on plumbing in rural England during the Victorian age with reference to the works of Charlotte M. Yonge. We have lunch together afterwards and you can tell us about your biography.'

40

'I am afraid I'm completely tied up on the 30th.' Hilary had no interest in Victorian plumbing.

'Then you must come and have supper with me tonight,' Moira said, determined that her 'find' should not disappear completely, 'and you can tell me all about your book. You must see that it is very exciting for us that someone is tackling the subject of Charlotte M. Yonge.'

'The thing is,' Hilary said, a little desperately, 'I don't think you will be very interested in what I am writing. You see, I always treat the subject (in this particular case Charlotte M. Yonge) as a floor plan. Once you have a floor plan, how you choose to use it is up to you. You might for instance place a carpet on the floor of your own design. Then on the carpet you might put a chair and if that looks nice you might, if you think it fits and fulfils the pattern that you intend the room to take, add a table. Then if the reader is lucky there may be a comforting cat curled up on the hearth. Or alternatively there might not.'

The three women looked at her blankly. There was nothing they could think of to say to Hilary Greep's approach to biography and to the life of Charlotte M. Yonge.

'Isn't that fascinating,' Moira said. 'You can tell me all about your floor plan over dinner,' and clasping Hilary's arm she took her away.

'I don't like the sound of that,' Katherine said.

'I'm sure Moira will tell us all about it on the 30th,' Maisy said drily.

Chapter Four

She had done it again. It had to be deliberate. A constricted feeling rose from her chest into her throat. Maisy Armstrong felt tears in her eyes. It was so unfair. How long had she been left here? She looked down at her swollen wrist. It was the third time this week that Laura had failed to put her watch on her. She had asked for it three times since breakfast! Nowadays if she failed to mention it as Laura dressed her, she spent the day without it. And it was so easy to forget, consumed as she was with misery and anger at being left indefinitely in bed. Then there was the roughness of Laura's dressing to contend with. It hadn't always been like that. The truth was Laura did not like old flesh. That was the trouble. That was the trouble with everything. And now, here she was, stuck on the lavatory. She must have been here at least half an hour. If she complained, Laura would say nonsense, it had only been seven minutes. It was so humiliating. And boring, boring . . . boring! The doorbell rang. Here she was stuck on the loo with the doorbell ringing. Who was it? Here she was stuck on the loo with *her* doorbell, not Laura's, *her doorbell* ringing. With a great effort she shifted her thighs a little, trying to relieve her flesh which was being cut into by the seat. It was not surprising that she was sometimes caught short and wet herself, as Laura was inclined to leave her for half an hour if she asked to go. She was old corrupt flesh, that was the trouble. She repelled herself as well as Laura. Nowadays when she brushed her hair, half her scalp seemed to come away. Did Laura think she liked to live like this? To be a burden? Who was at the door? She heard murmurings and then Laura came along the corridor. Nothing wrong with her hearing.

Laura appeared at the bathroom door. She was a slim woman with short brown hair in a gamine cut, brown, almond-shaped eyes and a soft clear complexion. She was looking pleasant. The cross sulky look was gone but her mother could tell it was pretence.

'John's here,' Laura said. 'He always seems to be popping round.' Crouching forward, taking Maisy's weight on her back, she pulled her mother up and handed her some lavatory paper (there were certain indignities spared them), pulled up her pants, smoothed her skirt over her hips and manhandled her into her wheelchair.

Seven minutes later they arrived smiling in the sitting-room to greet John. He bent down to kiss her. Maisy clutched at his arm, feeling the rock of his muscle.

'Are you all right, Mummy?' he asked, startled by the force of her fingers. She had never been particularly demonstrative.

'Fine,' she said, smiling. 'I'm just pleased to see you.'

Laura stood next to the wheelchair, smiling, her soft enigmatic smile. She had a pretty mouth. It and her eyes were her best features. In the past men had slept with her because of her mouth, late at night after parties.

Recently John had come to view her smile with unease.

Not that it had changed in any essential since she had sat in a pram, her infant face framed by a Liberty bonnet. For the last nine months, ever since Laura had stopped complaining about looking after their mother, he had felt mildly troubled by the two of them. It was probably guilt. His relief when his wife had said that she would prefer to leave rather than look after his mother had been profound. It had been an intractable problem. If his mother had been willing for them to liquidate all her assets they might – but only might – have afforded to have her looked after in a home, but she was mentally vigorous and up until now had deeply resented the suggestion that she should be tidied away. Since both his parents had been writers and their books were long out of print, there was no income from them. His mother lived on an annuity taken out when his father died. If Laura was to be released, a full-time nurse would have to be hired and he would have to pay for it. The recession had hit his architectural practice badly. He could not afford it. Hence his unease as he looked at his sister's smiling, threatening face.

'I've brought a book I thought you might like to read,' he said. 'You've probably seen the reviews. It's a biography of Mrs Gaskell. Maureen's just finished it and says it's terrific.' Maureen was his wife.

Maisy put out her hand. She was pleased. She had remarked its passage through the papers, and had thought of asking Laura for it as a birthday present. Her eighty-first birthday was only a fortnight away and Laura would be nice to her on her birthday. She had always taken birthdays seriously.

'How nice of you, John! I've never understood why she is considered to be a more serious writer than Charlotte M. Yonge. Perhaps it is because in biographical terms she had more of a life. The young today seem more interested in the life of a writer than in their works. They even interpret the

44

works in the light of the life, which in Charlotte M. Yonge's case is transparently impossible since all her papers were destroyed. I do thank you, I've been wanting to read it.'

'That reminds me,' Laura said. 'Katherine Sackville rang yesterday. She wanted to chat about Moira's lecture.'

'When? When did she ring?' Maisy asked sharply.

'I said yesterday.'

'When yesterday? Why did I not hear it? You must have known that I would have liked to talk to Katherine.'

'It was while you were in your bath. I don't know why you're making such a fuss; you can talk to Katherine any time you feel like lifting up the telephone receiver.'

Maisy remembered that bath. She had been left in it for about an hour and a half until the water was tepid and her skin crumpled. 'You should have told me,' she said, childish tears starting in her eyes.

'That reminds me, I ran into John Martin at the Garrick. He said you seemed to be lying low, that he had rung you half a dozen times and you hadn't returned his calls.' John did not add that was why he had come round.

Maisy looked at Laura.

'He rang twice,' she said.

Looking at the two of them, John felt the tension. His heart sank. 'How about some coffee?' he asked Laura.

Laura went to the kitchen.

'Look, I'll take time off and take you to your Chaplet of Pearls meeting the day after tomorrow.'

'If I'm up in time to go to it. You must ask Laura. As you know I cannot get up without her.'

John's anxiety increased. His stomach clenched and he felt in his jacket for an indigestion tablet.

*   *   *

45

Grace was visiting her husband Robert at the London Clinic. Her right hand was under the sheet while her pretty, tentative voice told him about the difficulties of the small house in Hillgate Street, Notting Hill Gate. One afternoon, nine months earlier, Grace had noticed movement under the bedclothes. Lifting them she had found Robert's penis raised to half-mast. The only other sign of consciousness was the restless movement of his eyeballs beneath his half-closed lids. Since his waving member must show some sort of consciousness, she decided to give him pleasure in the only way that seemed possible. Some days it worked and Robert would ejaculate over her hand. On others, like today, it remained soft and sad to her touch. Since she had discovered that he responded to her hand she could no longer be certain that he could not hear or even comprehend what was going on around him. She had once read a story called 'Duet of Death' by Hilda Lawrence about a woman who had a stroke after witnessing a murder and was unable to tell anyone while the murderer watched to see if she showed any sign of recovery. She thought it quite possible that Robert was lying there suffering agonies of boredom, and since she had long run out of conversation she sold the house in South Audley Street to have something to talk about. Now she told him how impossible Percy was as a cleaning woman, how she was rude and drunk. Illustrating her rudeness she told him how, making conversation, she had asked if Percy was her real name. Percy had replied that it was none of her business. She described Percy's long thin bony face, how her pink scalp showed through her wispy white hair, and how her false teeth as often as not were left by the kitchen sink. 'Apparently, when young, she was lady's maid to Lady Dunferlin and quite pretty. Katherine says she slept with everyone's husband. That's how everyone got to know her. But I don't see why I should have to employ her, do you? You didn't sleep with her, did you? I don't owe her, even if the others do.' She then told him how Katherine had insisted she give the lunch for the Pearls as usual, despite having moved to a tiny house and only having Percy to help – that is, when Percy condescended to turn up at all. 'I shall give them cucumber sandwiches and soup. Since Blanche had her stroke, Katherine has become very arrogant and bossy. They must learn that Notting Hill Gate is not South Audley Street.'

In the past the Pearls' meetings had always taken place in Grace's house in South Audley Street because it was generally considered since she had a full complement of servants that she would be the least put out. Grace had not viewed the matter in the same light. She considered that her friends took advantage of the fact that she did not work. But her habitual mewings of mild complaint about most things meant that her friends gave her utterances about as much attention as the background murmur of a brook. And anyway they liked eating smoked salmon, thin slices of beef in sauces and grapes glazed in sugar in a web of caramel, all sumptuously served on gold-rimmed plates.

As a young woman Grace had been gentle and exceptionally elegant. Neither clever nor ambitious, she was considered by her friends to be as aesthetically pleasing as a portrait by Sargent. Grace was universally liked and much sought after, as her non-emphatic beauty had led people to think she was their particular discovery. This had added glamour to unnecessary occasions such as tea at Fortnum's. Her friends thought her husband, an extremely rich merchant banker, exactly the right person for her. Though she had not read Charlotte M. Yonge as a child, she had come to enjoy her under the influence of Georgina Matheson, who had thrust the books upon her, then questioned her to make sure she had read them. Gradually, she had become hooked on the ones she dutifully read. Sweet in nature, Grace found most of her acquaintances bullying, but put up with it.

Portia and Archie travelled up to London on the five-thirty from Taunton to Paddington on the day before the meeting of The Chaplet of Pearls. They had, to the relief of Portia, a table for four between them. They sat side by side. Archie had the window seat and Portia tried to read. Dull guilt blinded her eyes to the page. Katherine had been furious when Portia had rung to tell her that she was bringing Archie with her. Not that she had said so. She had said, 'I think perhaps you'd better stay with Georgina. It really won't matter what Archie gets up to there.' And then she had asked what Portia intended to do with Archie while the meeting took place.

Portia replied, 'I was thinking that perhaps he could sit quietly in the corner.'

'Impossible!' Katherine had said.

Portia had tried to justify herself. 'I can't leave him behind, Katherine. Anna said she would look after him but she wouldn't. She would forget about him and just go off somewhere. Or take him with her in the car and just lose him, and he can't be left by himself.' She could not explain about how he went down to the village and exposed himself. Only the night before he had said to Anna when sitting next to her in the kitchen as she chopped parsley, 'Shall I show you my willy?'

'No, darling,' Anna had replied, moving his hands as they

fiddled at his flies. 'Let it stay nice and warm inside. It will feel much more comfy in there. How long has this been going on?' Anna had asked her.

Portia had concentrated on kneading the bread she was making. 'I'm not sure. He doesn't do it to me. Mrs Gilroy asked to see me about six months ago and said it was becoming a problem in the village and she thought I should know.'

'How did she phrase it?' Anna had asked, intrigued.

'Really, Anna!' Portia had said crossly, and managed to shift the subject away from Archie and his behaviour.

More, even, than annoying Katherine, her other overwhelming guilt was how *unfeeling* she felt towards Archie. She looked at him sitting there, not really bothering with what was happening out of the window. At any moment he might start trying to struggle to the door, saying he wanted to go home. She dreamed of him dying. She fantasised about Anna losing him and finding him curled up as though fast asleep covered in leaves in the wood. Then surely she would weep for him.

Pretending she was Anna, who found kindness towards her father easy, she took Archie's hand. It slipped like an eel from hers. His hands fluttered, moved, working at the air as his eyes alighted everywhere and nowhere out of the train window and around the carriage. She was dead wood to him, Portia thought. Anna wasn't. None of the children were. Even if he did not recognise them, he responded to them. Even his visits to the villagers, knocking on their doors and exposing himself, had meaning for him of some sort. She was merely a hedge, a fence, a locked door. If that. He blindly obeyed her but she was not his friend. She felt desolation. He saw through her joyless care of him.

She tried to shift her unhappiness sideways, and thought of Anna. She was worried about Anna. At least when she was married her shiftlessness had been contained. Now it was striding out, covering ground. Portia did not like the elderly American businessman in whose large flat Anna had kept her suitcase, and who now had thrown her out because of the freedom with which she spent his money. Of course Anna *was* a spendthrift. Portia did not know where she got it from. Neither she nor Archie were, and whatever their numerous faults, neither were the other children. She had tried talking to Anna. She knew that being a kept woman was an old-fashioned concept, but that was what Anna was. Anna had tried to defend herself by saying all married women were kept women and anyway, she liked being a kept woman. She had to get the black bread and margarine from somewhere! Not that Portia had used the term 'kept woman'; it had been Anna who had called herself that. Portia had merely said that Anna's life was unsatisfactory and rackety.

'Why don't you get married if you want to be together?' she asked.

'Darling, you would hate me to marry him, you know you would. He would probably think he owned me and expect me to stay in and cook for him. And anyway, if I were to do it again it would be to marry a peer. Wouldn't you like me to marry a lord? Marrying Chase wouldn't be romantic,' Anna said.

Portia remembered her daughter Eliza telling her how she had stayed with Anna and Chase on a visit to London. Anna had come dancing into the sitting-room one evening crying, 'I'm having dinner with a lord, Chase, a lord. What do you think of that!' While Chase slouched in his chair glumly looking at television.

'Don't be silly!' Portia was cross.

'Anyway, until now I've liked living with Chase. Although

50

he *is* becoming more and more difficult. He's obsessed with money. It's so silly. He's disgustingly rich. He's creepy with it, hoarding it up and shouting and yelling just because I over-spent on the gold card. It's impossible not to spend money if you have a gold card.'

'Is it his gold card?'

'It's my gold card but it comes out of his account.'

Portia was horrified. 'Why doesn't he give you house-keeping money once a month? That would give you something to work to.'

'He's away quite a lot. He likes to be able to check up on me. This way if I go off with someone divine to Greece or somewhere, he can tell.'

'And you say that is better than marriage.' Portia was astounded.

'It's not much different. Charles used to twist my arms to find out where I'd gone and who with. Personally I prefer a gold card.'

Before arriving at Paddington she sewed up Archie's flies in the lavatory. There might be an accident but that was a lesser worry.

Georgina was mildly annoyed with Portia when she rang asking if she could come to stay for the meeting, and bring Archie. She was fond of Portia but as she said to Georgio, 'It is typical of Portia to insist on bringing Archie, demonstrating her burden to us. She can't just let go and have fun. She wouldn't have come unless she'd contrived to make it uncomfortable for herself. Portia has spent her life expiating some unconscious sin. It's a great mistake to believe in sin. Percy will have to look after Archie when we meet at Grace's, that is, unless you . . .'

51

'No,' said Georgio.

'Percy will know what to do. She can take him for a walk in the park. Apparently he's still as active as a monkey. He used to be called Twinkle-toes because of his dancing. That's how he got Portia. He caught her on the dance floor in a moment of guilt-free, mindless happiness.'

Annabel Butler Moore lived in a small house in Lawrence Street in Chelsea. It had been a pretty, airy house but in recent months a medicinal smell pervaded it. Annabel nowadays slept in the sitting-room, which saved her the ordeal of climbing the stairs. She no longer thought to draw the curtains back, and the unlit blue-and-white room now seemed gloomy. Mainly because movement was painful, she had gradually succumbed to receiving visitors propped up on her bed. Her daughter Clare had installed an entry-phone buzzer, which lay on her pillow. Now she no longer needed to struggle to the door when visitors came to see her. She did however make the painful effort of dressing every day.

This Thursday, the day before the meeting of The Chaplet of Pearls, Katherine was visiting her. As she arrived she pulled back the curtains and opened the window. 'That's better!' she said. If they were to have a good time together she had to pretend, at least to herself, that Annabel was merely suffering from flu.

Annabel smiled acceptance of Katherine's desire to command. 'Have you brought the itinerary?' she asked.

Katherine sat by her bed and ate the grapes she had brought Annabel. 'Yes, you will come, won't you? I'll pick you up and if it becomes too tiring for you, we'll call you a taxi. Portia is coming.'

'Let's see how I am tomorrow. I'd like to come.' She quickly stroked Katherine's hand and then withdrew her own. She had shrunk to birdlike proportions in the last few months and was incredibly thin.

Katherine sometimes thought that Annabel would die from knocking herself against something and shattering into porcelain-like shards rather than from the slow cancer eating her up. 'Grace is playing hostess and moaning about it as usual. She has nothing else to do except visit Robert at the London Clinic. She's in danger of addling her brain. It's a pity both her children live abroad. She needs some kind of irritant to jangle her up. I've sent her Percy who seems to be doing quite a good job of annoying her,' she said.

'You're full of tender loving care,' Annabel jeered.

'I know. I surprise myself!'

Annabel changed the subject. 'Nancy Tregunter came yesterday. It was sweet of her. Her legs are really not so good nowadays. She brought me *Bleak House* on tape. Because of the drugs I can't really concentrate to read any more. I didn't tell her but I won't listen to it. The end must be quite near now. I can't be bothered with fiction. It can't be right, can it, to read yourself into death? Unless of course it's a religious book and you believe in God and the hereafter. Do you believe in the hereafter and God?'

'I don't think so,' Katherine said. 'Do you?'

'No, I don't think so. Although when I read the papers I want to believe in hell. I don't think it's fair that real wickedness and cruelty should go unpunished like the IRA or youths who torture and kill the likes of us, and then I have always minded terribly about Outer Mongolia. Since there is little punishment on earth, I think I believe in hell.'

'I think the Jews have got it right. They don't have to believe in God unless they want to, but they believe you should exact a tooth for a tooth and an eye for an eye. Since the death of God and morality, and the conception of right and wrong, and the belief that the courts will see justice done, all that is left is an eye for an eye and a tooth for a tooth.'

'It takes years to become a Jew. Neither of us has that much time left.'

'I know, but in the way some people are vaguely Christian, I think I am vaguely Jewish.'

'What do you still care about, Katherine?' There was something judgemental in Annabel's gaze.

'I can't really say at the moment. Caring about something hits you like a thunderbolt and I haven't felt a thunderbolt for a very long time.'

'Perhaps feeling has withered with our flesh.'

'Oh, I don't think so,' Katherine said. 'I think feeling, emotion, caring, whatever you call it, is the last thing to go. I think I'm just waiting for a thunderbolt.'

Maisy was in a reverie when Katherine rang her at seven o'clock that evening. She always felt hungry as a lion by seven. In the last few years she had found that she thought more about food than she used to. Perhaps because there was less to occupy her thoughts than when she was more active. Laura said that she had become greedy and that it was unhealthy in an inactive woman to eat large meals three times a day. Sometimes she only gave her bread and soup out of a tin for supper. Maisy wanted to sink her uncertain teeth into meat. She was thinking about meat and gravy and potatoes when the telephone rang.

'Have you heard? Portia is bringing Archie up for the meeting.' Katherine's voice was exasperated. 'Isn't it intolerable!'

'Poor Archie!' Maisy said perfunctorily and then added with malicious intent, 'Perhaps Laura could look after him. After all, she knows the ropes; she looks after me.'

'Percy is to take him for a walk.'

'She will probably sexually abuse him.'

They both cackled.

'See you tomorrow.' Katherine rang off.

Of course Maisy knew she would see Katherine tomorrow even though Laura had not admitted the feasibility of the outing as yet. She had a slightly wheezy cough and every time she mentioned the meeting Laura said they must see how she was on the day. Laura's cruelties were not premeditated. They were spontaneous to the occasion. Since John was delivering her to the meeting she was unlikely to put a stop to it but still Maisy felt nervous. Why was Laura cruel? She thought of Laura as a little girl. Had Laura, as she played God with her dolls, smacked and punished them? Maisy could not remember. Why could she not remember? After all, she only had two children. You would have thought she would remember what they were like. She remembered John when little very distinctly. He was sweet and liked being cuddled. Why was Laura's babyhood so dim? She could hardly have muddled her with any other little girl. She closed her eyes, squeezing them shut. Laura as a little girl. Laura curled up on David's lap. Always David's lap. Very pretty, very self-contained. Hated little boys aged seven. One for the bushes when she was fifteen. She had always been Daddy's little girl and of course there had been ructions when she had discovered boys. David had not liked it. And she, to be honest, had not liked the way David had not liked it. Laura had always been an icy little queen, accepting his gifts as her due. He had started giving her jewellery from an early age. Really pretty little things he came across in junk shops. Perfectly suitable: little bracelets of beaten silver, a necklace of seed pearls, another of little flowers made from some pink semi-precious stones. Then there were rings when she was a little older. He gave them just when he felt like it, not just on birthdays and Christmas. She had not approved but had said nothing. Laura had been spoilt by David, Maisy thought, and she was still spoilt and selfish. So she was unmarried. A spinster. Nobody had measured up to Daddy. A spoilt life, and she took it out on her.

Chapter Five

The day of the meeting was gusty and overcast. The members clustered slightly uncomfortably in Grace's small sitting-room with its too large furniture. Georgina and Portia had arrived late because Archie had a little accident shortly before they set out. Georgina was feeling cross. The seat of one of her armchairs had been made disagreeably wet and would, despite Portia's efforts with washing-up liquid, smell when dry. Why could Archie not wear a nappy like others with his problem? Perhaps Portia did not care what happened to the armchairs down at Sheldon Hall, but she should have better manners than to import her eccentric life to London. She adjusted her hearing aid which screeched horribly.

Grace offered everybody coffee or sherry. They opted for sherry as being less time-consuming. After regretting absent members, it was eleven-thirty when Moira introduced Katherine's lecture to the remaining four (Bad Annabel had not been well enough to come). Given to puns she made mention of how Katherine's lecture on Plumbing in Rural England Between 1848 and 1870 with Reference to the Works of Charlotte M. Yonge would undoubtedly plumb the depths of Victorian plumbing.

Grace tittered politely.

Katherine read her paper. It showed how the effects of bad drainage or no drainage at all had affected the lives of the poor. These had been vividly described by Charlotte M. Yonge in her novel *The Young Stepmother*. Albinia, the principal character and the young stepmother in question, not only had to contend with her three stepchildren's decidedly common accents and thought processes, but also with a husband who suffered from melancholic lethargy brought about by the Indian climate and the deaths of his silly young first wife and a beloved first-born son from typhus. Albinia is convinced that their deaths are attributable to bad drainage. The village's bad drainage is at the heart of the novel and not until Albinia succeeds in improving the characters of both husband and stepchildren does the village become a model of modern sanitation.

There was much discussion and some digression after Katherine had finished reading her paper before the subject turned to Hilary Greep. 'She says,' Moira explained, 'that Charlotte M. Yonge is a floor plan and that it is up to her as the writer to make the best of the plan that she can. What she proposes to put into the empty space is the idea that Miss Yonge was sexually abused by her father.'

Her statement was greeted by a startled silence.

Grace broke it. 'Oh dear! Do you think it could be true?'

'What evidence did she produce?' Katherine asked.

'None.'

'Didn't you ask?'

'Of course I asked. She said that Yonge – she calls her Yonge – that Yonge was a dysfunctional adult, unnaturally attached to male authority, and that although her intellect had developed to embrace such things as languages, history and nature studies, emotionally she was a pre-adolescent child attached to Daddy and religion. She said it is clear from her novels that she was abused. I asked, what novels? And then she mentioned *Nutty's Father*.'

'What about *Nutty's Father*?' Georgina asked.

'I'm afraid I didn't take in what she was saying. My mind was in a whirl. I have to say, despite being a very liberated writer – my publisher has sometimes found it necessary to edit my sex scenes – I was greatly shocked. For a few minutes I stopped thinking.'

'Is *Nutty's Father* about sexual abuse?' Grace asked in bewilderment.

'Of course not,' Maisy said.

Georgina explained. (She rarely felt impatient with Grace.) 'It's the story of a pretty widow and her teenage daughter Nutty, who live a happy, religiously fulfilling life in the country until it is discovered that Nutty's father, a dissolute aristocrat given to opium and debauchery, is still alive. Before Nutty was born he had abandoned her mother whom he met when she was a seventeen-year-old governess. He had intended only to seduce her but instead found himself married. As the plot unfolds, the family is reunited and Nutty's mother spends the rest of her life wearing herself out looking after her husband and trying to arrest his physical and spiritual degeneration. Nutty hates and despises him but, when her mother dies of exhaustion in childbirth, she sacrifices her youth to the demands of a selfish and disgusting old man. At the end, she marries an elderly manufacturer of umbrellas who had carried a torch for her mother when he had thought her a widow.'

'I remember the story perfectly well,' Grace said crossly.

'I was enquiring whether there was sexual abuse in it because I could not remember any.'

'Well, there isn't.'

'What is she like?' Maisy asked.

'She's very young and quite pretty but doesn't make the best of herself,' Moira replied. 'A bit on the droopy side. She wears heavy leather booties and long cotton dresses.'

'That's not quite what I mean. I did see her the other night. If we took her up and pointed out her errors, would she be amenable?'

'I'm not sure she looks on errors in quite the same light as we do. She seems to think it an advantage that Charlotte Yonge's papers were destroyed. Also, she already has a publisher for the book.'

'But nobody gets published nowadays,' Maisy exclaimed in dismay.

'You do if you write tosh,' Katherine said. 'And it seems she does.'

'Oh what a pity Blanche is unconscious. I'm sure she would have known what we should do,' Grace said.

Katherine ignored her. 'We must have her to a meeting. Until we know exactly what she is up to it is impossible to decide what we should do.'

'We're not due to meet for another six months. By then, for all we know, her manuscript might be with a publisher,' Moira pointed out.

'We must meet again soon, in two or three weeks. Moira: you invite her. And cultivate her.'

'I can't. I'm going home the day after tomorrow.'

'This is too important. You must cancel your flight. Until we settle how to deal with the matter you must remain here. You are our link with her.'

'You don't understand,' Moira wailed. 'I can't possibly stay. I'm giving a cocktail party two days after I get back, and then there are my plants and my cat. I simply can't stay.'

'You have to,' Katherine said fiercely. 'How would you like it if someone wrote an article saying your father had abused you and that accounted for the fact that you were an unmarried old . . .' She stopped just in time and substituted 'lesbian' for 'soak'.

'That is quite impossible. My affairs are legendary.'

'Katherine's right. You must cancel your drinks party,' Maisy said.

'Yes, you must,' the others said in chorus.

Moira felt harassed. 'I will see what can be done. I am a very busy woman. You probably don't realise this because you see me on my holidays.'

'You must stay here indefinitely until this biography has been dealt with,' Katherine said, and added, 'I think we should ask Miss Greep to address the meeting on her insight into Miss Yonge. That should give us a fair idea of what we are up against. Anyway, it would be impossible for one of us to carry out the necessary research for a lecture in a fortnight.'

'Quite impossible,' they agreed.

'Moira, it is up to you to make her come.'

Grace's sandwiches were eaten with some backward thoughts to the days of cooks and uniformed maids. Maisy felt unable to drink anything. The only bathroom was up a steep flight of stairs. Even if there had been a lavatory on the ground floor she would have hated to have asked any of them for help. As it was she was in severe discomfort when Laura came to fetch her at three o'clock. By then the gathering had mostly dispersed as Percy had rung from a pub in Lancaster Gate to say she had lost Archie.

It was a few days after the Pearls' meeting that Laura had dinner at John's house. An agency nurse was spending the evening with Maisy. Maureen, John's wife, had left the room ostensibly to make coffee but really to leave the two of them alone so that John could criticise Laura without her. Maureen quite liked Laura and felt mildly guilty that she had landed her with Maisy.

'Mummy seems unhappy,' John said. 'Why?'

'I expect because she's old.'

'She's been old for ages. I thought that perhaps the two of you were not getting on at the moment.'

Laura ignored his comment. 'Being old is an unhappy condition. Being in a wheelchair is an unhappy condition. Being dressed, manhandled and put to bed is an unhappy condition. Of course she's unhappy. I've never really understood why babies put up with it. I expect they blot it out as soon as they can and then resent all those ghastly photographs of themselves splayed out on a rug with nothing on.'

'It's more than that.'

'We never have got on particularly well.'

'That's nonsense.'

'It isn't. She despises me for not having married. She thinks because I am not married I have failed with men. And she is one of those women who think that to fail with men is to fail in life.'

'Bullshit.' John spoke with vigour because he also believed his sister had failed to make anything of her life. A spinster secretary to a dim Conservative MP could hardly claim to have made a satisfactory go of things.

'She feels contempt for me as a woman who has failed where she succeeded. Ever since I was a baby she has seen me as a rival, and now she thinks of me as a rival who has lost out. She thinks I am neutered because I am not married. She is incapable of contemplating the idea that a woman can be sexual without marrying. Mummy thinks that a woman's role is to batten on to men. She is male oriented. She cared for you and Daddy and that was it.'

'You're talking nonsense. She always loved you just as much as me.'

'She thinks a single woman is a poor thing. She thinks it is my duty to look after her. She does not think that through love or affection I might actually wish to do so, but simply that because I am unmarried I *should* do so. Just as you do.'

'Of course I don't.' John spoke heatedly.

'Because I am female and unmarried you consider that my life is of no account.' Laura's voice was loaded with emotion. 'Why should *my* life be sacrificed? Why should you and Maureen not *share* the burden of Mother? Do you know or care what is happening to me?'

'Stop it. I want to talk about Mother. Every time I try to do so you talk about yourself. Let's discuss Mummy. Not you. Mummy.' He strove to modulate his voice. 'Let's discuss why she is unhappy and what should be done about it.'

Laura ignored him. 'I'm forty-nine. My hair has quite suddenly gone limp. My skin is drying up. I feel the *prune* trying to assert itself upon my bones. My menstrual cycle is in chaos – don't look like that! For more than fifty per cent of the population it is one of the most fundamental facts of living – it gave birth to you. I suffer from night sweats in which my mind is filled with images of decay. *And at this point* in my life you decide that I should look after the end product of all this – Mother!'

'Oh for Christ's sake! Maureen's fifty and she doesn't go on like this.'

'No. She doesn't want to revolt you.'

'Poor Mummy. So you bully her.'

Laura's expression stilled. 'I don't.'

'You do.'

'Does she say I do?'

'No, but she wouldn't. She's humiliated by not being in control of things.'

'Why shouldn't you look after her?' Laura asked passionately.

'We've been through all that. The fact that you are unmarried and that your employer lost his seat does have a bearing on things. You don't have a job, commitments, or dependants.'

'An experienced MP's secretary can always get another job in the Commons.'

'There are four of us whose lives would be adversely affected if we had Mummy living with us. And the fact is, Maureen has never liked her. It simply wouldn't work.'

'I don't like her either. I never have. Ever.'

'That's a lie. I don't believe you.'

'I never have. Not ever. Even as a child. I probably have loved her sometimes. It is even possible I still do. But I have never liked her and you can't live with someone you don't like. The only time love becomes more important than liking is in sex. Then, of course, people are landed with – and put up with – the most ghastly partners.'

'Maureen doesn't like her and she's not related to her. She simply won't do it, and I don't see why she should,' John said

64

slowly. 'But if she did, she wouldn't go around moaning about her drying skin. She gets on with life. She always has and you haven't, and that's what your complaints are really about.'

'Maureen lives in disguise. She probably thinks that if she really told you how she felt you would go out and get a mistress.'

John already had one. 'Stop it! This is absurd. If you are as antagonistic to Mummy as you appear to be we will have to find another solution.'

'You mean you will have her here?'

'No. I told you Maureen won't. She will have to move to a home or have a live-in nurse who won't bully her.'

'I don't bully her.'

'You do.'

Laura wept. She wept from rage, despair, and because she was abandoning her mother.

Chapter Six

Hilary looked at the six old women assembled to meet her in Annabel Butler Moore's house in Chelsea. She had come reluctantly. Moira had told her that The Chaplet of Pearls had come into possession of the letters that Charlotte M. Yonge wrote to the invalidish Mrs Keble during her lifetime, and that they would allow her to see them if she would consent to lunch with the Pearls, and tell them about her work on the biography. It was always possible that the letters might throw unexpected light on Yonge's relationship with John Keble.

She found herself not looking at the bed on which her hostess lay. She had been warned by Moira Lockheart what to expect but still found it difficult not to stare. Against the protests of the nurse and Annabel Katherine had opened the windows wide but there was still a fusty, medicinal smell to the room.

The Pearls had decided to meet around Bad Annabel's bed as it seemed important that they should all be there to confront the crisis. Dressed and made-up Annabel lay propped against plumped-up pillows on her bed. Her heroin drip was discreetly hidden from view beneath a handkerchief. The nurse had taken the opportunity to go out and do

66

some essential shopping. Annabel had explained that they would almost certainly require lunch and had suggested to the nurse, a jolly, beefy New Zealand girl called Jane, that she bring some smoked-salmon sandwiches from the local delicatessen. The sandwiches would not be as good as home-made ones: the delicatessen used margarine and thick, soft bread embedded with bits of grain that got stuck between teeth. But they would do.

Hilary smiled. She felt unexpectedly shy and awkward. Moira took charge of her, taking her hand and squeezing it. She led her round, introducing her. 'This is Annabel Butler Moore, our hostess.'

Annabel raised an insect arm and said, 'Welcome. We love to meet fellow admirers of Miss Yonge.'

Hilary's hand remained safely encased in Moira's damp enclosure. She had never seen anyone as ill as Annabel before. She was shocked into stillness.

'And this is the well-known biographer, Maisy Armstrong.'

'We met the other evening,' Maisy said, shaking hands. 'We have been looking forward to hearing about your biography.'

'How do you do.' Hilary was glad to regain her voice and her hand. She kept the latter to herself after that, bowing from the waist at each introduction. She was dressed in three layers of gun-metal grey things, the longest of which reached her ankles, and was beginning to feel quite hot.

'We often invite a guest speaker,' Annabel explained, 'and what Moira told us about your approach to Charlotte M. Yonge has interested us beyond anything.'

'We hoped you might be prepared to address us,' Georgina added.

'I'm not sure I want to lecture to so many experts on Yonge.

I'd be afraid of making a fool of myself. I'd hoped this might be more of an exchange of information and ideas. I'm sure you all know much more about the subject of her life than I do.'

'The subject of her life?' Katherine said in a musing, querying tone, and then giving the words an equal emphasis, repeated, 'The subject of her life.' And then again, 'The subject of her life. It's strange how the meaning of a phrase can go astray when repeated. What would you say the words meant? I mean, if you had said, "I am sure you all know much more about her life than I do," we would all know exactly what the words meant. Not, of course, that we necessarily do know more about her,' and she smiled at Hilary.

'I wasn't being careless, if that's what you thought.'

'I didn't think you were. That is what makes it so interesting.'

Portia touched Hilary on her arm. 'Do sit down. This isn't an inquisition, you know. It's just that we are very interested in the works of Charlotte M. Yonge and it is fascinating to have discovered someone so young who is both an enthusiast and actually going to write about her.'

'And now that we are all sitting comfortably, shall we begin?' Moira suggested. In her youth Moira had once written a story for the radio programme *Listen with Mother*.

Nobody picked up the reference.

Sometimes, Katherine thought, Moira was almost as silly as Grace.

'It is not of primary importance to me whether Charlotte M. Yonge was a wonderful writer, merely a good one, or actually bad,' Hilary explained. 'Writing called "good" – canonisation – is writing which a society has deemed good for a particular reason. Crudely, I belong to a branch of women's studies that approaches the past, whether it be art or literature, for what it tells us about the society that produced it. In effect, we recontextualise the product. For instance, at the moment, when this kind of feminist art historian looks at a picture she is not interested in whether a painting is good, how the paint was applied, the originality of the subject matter, or even the conscious intentions of the painter. She is interested in the sub-text of the painting, the things the painter had no idea she or he was showing – their unconscious prejudices. The same with the novel. We are no longer interested in literature as literature – "fine writing" – or the intentions of the writer. We are interested in the novel's sub-text. We are as interested in contextualising what is written on a beer mat as we are in learning what George Eliot thought she was up to when writing *Silas Marner*. Charlotte M. Yonge's novels could be beer mats. I am merely going one step further when treating Yonge herself as a beer mat, a sub-text. That is why she is the subject of the life.'

'I see,' Katherine said slowly. 'So you are not in fact an admirer of Charlotte M. Yonge?'

'Well, I wouldn't go so far as to say that. I have found a number of her novels riveting – I am sure, for many of the same reasons that you do.'

'I doubt it.' Georgina was so fierce that proceedings were brought to a startled and awkward pause.

'I think sherry might be in order,' Annabel suggested. 'Grace, you couldn't go to the kitchen and see if Jane has prepared a tray with glasses and a decanter?'

It's always me, Grace thought as she left the room. Nobody would ever dream of sending Katherine to bring in the drinks tray.

She found Jane in the kitchen unwrapping some unattractive-looking sandwiches.

'How's it going?' Jane asked.

'Not very well. A bit tricky.' She eyed the large, awkward-looking tray with misgiving. She was wearing heels and could imagine herself toppling forward with it. She grasped the tray unconvincingly and raised it with a deliberate swaying motion.

'You go back. I'll bring it through,' Jane said.

What a nice girl, Grace thought. Perhaps she should have Robert home and have a nice Jane to look after him. Perhaps he would prefer it. At the thought, panic loosened the walls around her, leaving her exposed and frightened. She saw Robert's still, uncommunicative body lying in a hospital bed on a drip in her spare bedroom upstairs. His presence an alien, heavy silence invading the house. How could she sit downstairs watching television, reading a book or enjoying a glass of sherry while he lay upstairs thinking or not thinking, being or not being. It was better for him to be in the clinic with the bustle all around and the clink of things going by in the passage, and faces popping in and out. And then he had her visits to look forward to with the secret pleasure that they shared. Anyway, he would hate the new house. It wasn't what he was used to.

She returned with Jane. Moira poured the sherry. Annabel accepted a glass but as usual did not touch it.

'Now tell us more about your book.' Moira moved her chair closer to Hilary and patted her hand. After all, Hilary was her discovery and she wanted, like any proud keeper of a circus animal, to show off all the terrible facets of this new and dangerous creature.

Hilary rummaged in her carrier bag for a file. 'I have come partially prepared. I think the easiest way of explaining my approach to the life of Charlotte M. Yonge is to read you a piece from the feminist writer Andrea Dworkin's book, *Right-Wing Women*. In it she describes how men reduce women to being' – Hilary, instinctively protective, spared them the words 'pussy' and 'cunt' – 'a vagina and womb. She says that women have been so conditioned by men that the prostitute will defend the pimp, finding her worth in the light cast by his macho pride, and that the housewife will defend the husband who anchors her to a lifetime of servitude to his needs. For a woman to question the ideology that has led to her enslavement would mean, and I quote, that "all the ideals that motivated her to deny herself would be indelibly stained with blood that she would have to acknowledge, at last, as her own".' Hilary stopped reading and looked up. 'And it is here that what Andrea has to say is of particular relevance to the life and works of Yonge.' She quoted:

So the woman hangs on, not with the delicacy of a clinging vine, but with a tenacity incredible in its intensity, to the very persons, institutions, and values that demean her, degrade her, glorify her powerlessness, insist upon constraining and paralysing the most honest expressions of her will and being. She becomes a lackey, serving those who ruthlessly and effectively aggress against her and her kind. This singularly self-hating loyalty to those committed to her own destruction is the very essence of womanhood as men of all ideological persuasions define it.

She stopped and looked at them.

There was a pause while her audience tried to work out the relevance of the passage to the life and work of their heroine.

71

'We are, of course, aware that Miss Yonge subjugated her own instincts and wishes and those of her female characters to the authority of the male, but don't you think that you are over-stating it a bit?' Maisy enquired mildly. 'There are also male characters who subdue their inclinations to what Miss Yonge considered right. And her main interest in presenting a picture of male authority at the head of the family is in the sacred preservation of the family. She saw the two as indivisible from the Church of England (male) and the congregation (the family of the Church). The springs of her nature and of her writing were religious. God created the world and into the world He put a family. And so that that family might know Him, He came down from heaven, died on the cross, and after some vicissitudes the Church of England arose out of the darkness as a vehicle for the family to show its deep appreciation and awareness of Him. Blanche would have put it better.'

'Yonge was a lackey,' Hilary said. 'I would go even further – Yonge's religion propped her life up, because she was incapable of throwing off the yoke of her father's tyranny and needed some way to justify her subjection to his will. She was in physical and psychological bondage to him.'

Invisible to her unknowing eye, a rustle as restless as wintry leaves on dry twigs ran through the Pearls. They were getting closer to the charge of incest!

'*Nutty's Father*!' Grace exclaimed, amazed at her insight into what Hilary had been saying.

Hilary looked at the watery-eyed, skinny woman with the dyed-blonde wispy bun who had half risen out of her chair in excitement. She had not really noticed her before. She looked like a desiccated hare. 'Well, yes. *Nutty's Father* is the key to understanding a great deal about Yonge's psychological wounds and how she failed to deal with them. But there are clues and indications sprinkled lavishly throughout her work.'

'Do tell us how *Nutty's Father* implies that Mr Yonge had sex with his daughter,' Annabel said.

'I think we are moving a little too fast and that it would be better to have lunch now, if Annabel doesn't object,' Katherine suggested to the irritation of the others. She thought that tempers might run high when the discussion got under way and this might be the only opportunity of learning more about Hilary Greep's background and weaknesses. If they were to sabotage the book, the more they knew about her the better.

'Grace, you couldn't be very kind and see what's happening in the kitchen, could you?' Annabel asked.

'I'll go,' Moira said, getting up. 'I want to go to the loo anyway.'

'You might be more comfortable going to the bathroom upstairs. There is rather a lot of paraphernalia in the one down here.'

Always curious, Moira glanced into the downstairs bathroom on her way upstairs and was immediately stricken. A curious contraption was attached to the seat of the lavatory to enable Annabel to sit at the smallest possible incline and there was a rail on both sides to help her lower herself and rise again. It was sometimes possible to forget the pain that Annabel lived with as she lay in bed, smiling and engaging in conversation. This was a reminder of her drawn-out agony as she inched towards death. Moira saw herself sitting in her own light, pretty drawing-room in her villa in Saint-Barthélemy, a delicious sundowner at her elbow, looking out through the open french doors on to her sunny terrace. Life!

73

She closed the door, and after visiting the upstairs bathroom went along to the kitchen. Jane had disappeared somewhere but on the table lay a tray with a plate of sandwiches, wine glasses and two open bottles of white wine. We'll get covered in crumbs, she thought disapprovingly, seeing no plates. Like Grace before her she looked with disfavour at the tray. Picking up the bottles of wine she returned to the sitting-room.

'I need somebody for the glasses,' she said.

Katherine went back to the kitchen with her. 'We must find out as much as possible about Hilary. Interests, boyfriends, parents, where she studied, what she has published, medical situation, any madness in the family, all that sort of thing.'

'All right. Leave it to me. I feel quite like the aunt of the black sheep.' Moira hunted through the cupboards and found plates which she handed to Katherine. 'I would have made rather a good aunt. It's a pity I was an only child. If I had nieces or a nephew I could leave them all my money instead of having to do a yearly review of charities and trusts and things. By the way, I have cut out the RSPCA on your instructions because of the unnatural stand they take on hunting, but I decided it would be going a little too far to leave money to the hunting lobby. I don't think my fans would like it. They might be shocked.'

'Who *are* you leaving your money to?' Katherine enquired as they entered the sitting-room.

Moira was leaving most of her money to a trust that would present a prize for the best historical novel of the year. There would be three judges – an academic, an historical fiction writer and an eminent somebody. It would be called the Lockheart Prize and the proud winner would win £750. The winner would be announced at a slap-up, sit-down dinner for fifty people costing £2,500 and there would be an obligatory

74

toast to Moira Lockheart at the end of the meal. Before the meal the guests would be served a specially invented cocktail called the Lockheart Cocktail.

As they ate the spongy sandwiches, rather half-heartedly, Moira asked Hilary, 'My dear, do tell us about your family. Do you have lots of siblings beavering away in academia like yourself?'

'Well, I suppose you could say so.'

'How many of you are there?'

'Well, my primary nurturers were Andrea Dworkin and Mary Daly and my sisters are Susan Brownmiller and Susan Faludi.'

There was a pause while the Pearls tried to work out what she was on about.

Grace said, 'Two Susans in the same family must be rather difficult.'

Then Katherine asked, 'Not Germaine Greer?'

'No.'

'How about Simone de Beauvoir?' Maisy, who had looked on her as a great heroine in her youth, enquired.

'Great grandmother.' Hilary was enjoying herself.

'Grandmother?'

'Simone Weil.'

'Two Simones! And on the mother's side, I expect. That must be awkward.' Georgina looked at Grace slyly as she spoke.

'Perhaps there is a Welsh connection,' Maisy suggested. 'After all, until quite recently they were all called Llewellyn the son of Llewellyn the son of Llewellyn.' Being beastly to Grace was becoming a habit.

Katherine said, 'Goodness what a pedigree! Are there no men involved?'

75

'Artificial insemination has put paid to that.'

'I don't understand,' Grace said. 'Artificial insemination still involves male sperm.'

Katherine recited:

> My mother groan'd, my father wept,
> Into the dangerous world I leapt;
> Helpless, naked, piping loud:
> Like a fiend hid in a cloud.
>
> Struggling in my father's hands,
> Striving against my swaddling bands,
> Bound and weary I thought best
> To sulk upon my mother's breast.

'I hadn't quite thought of it like that,' Hilary said.

'A very useful poem. It's extraordinary how apt it is to different circumstances.'

'Are you Welsh?' Grace asked Hilary.

'No. I'm cosmopolitan.'

'How about your boyfriend? Perhaps he's Welsh?' Recklessly, Moira was moving on to question two.

Hilary blushed, very, very slightly. 'We, by that I mean my friends, decided celibacy is best.'

Surprise tripped Moira into warmth. 'How sensible!'

'Moira told us that you were studying Charlotte M. Yonge for a Ph.D. as well as writing a biography of her. Which university are you attached to?' Collecting plates Katherine looked around for somewhere to put them, and handed them to Grace who was still sitting down.

'Birkbeck College.'

'Oh! I once taught there. It obviously hasn't changed much.'

'What did you teach?' Hilary asked.

'Economic history. It's an interesting subject but never quite flew on its own. They would probably do better with it in an American institution. Are we having coffee?'

'Oh yes,' they all said.

'If you go into the hall and call for Jane, I'm sure she would not mind making it. She knows how to work the machine,' Annabel said.

'You couldn't ask her at the same time if she would mind helping me to the bathroom,' Maisy asked Katherine.

'And you could take these plates out.' Grace handed them back to her.

Over coffee the Pearls returned to the subject of *Nutty's Father*.

'When the story opens,' Hilary reminded them, 'Nutty is a rather immature, lively eighteen year old living in genteel but happy poverty with her mother and great aunt. She believes her father is dead and intends to teach for her living in the local school. She has grown up under the benign eye of a neighbour, Mr Dutton, a bachelor who is in love with her gentle mother. Significantly, Mr Dutton is a manufacturer of umbrellas.' Hilary paused. She hoped she would not need to explain the significance of umbrellas in the novel.

Her audience looked at her with blank expectation.

'I think Yonge's unconscious decision to make Mr Dutton an umbrella manufacturer will become clear,' she said firmly, hastening to move on. 'Then, quite suddenly, it turns out Nutty's mother is not a widow. This disgusting upper-class roué, who had abandoned her mother before she was born under pressure from his family, turns up to claim her. Nutty is expelled from her suburban paradise. She has to go and live with this disgusting old selfish reprobate in a large house where she is considered a hobbledehoy. Worse, she has to watch her mother being worn down trying to reclaim him from drugs.'

'We do know the novel,' Maisy said.

Georgina took up the story. 'Her mother dies giving birth to a baby after making Nutty promise to take care of the ghastly old man. Nutty puts aside her anger and dislike, tames her personality to dullness, and is half rescued by marrying the umbrella man.'

'Deconstructed this is a Jekyll and Hyde story of the good and bad father,' Hilary explained, 'in which the good father has sex with the daughter. It would have been impossible at that date to have allowed the real father to do it. Instead she gives the real father all the attributes of an abuser but allows her mother's would-be lover and her own would-be father the privilege of possession. You can plainly see her unconscious at work. On a conscious level Yonge loves her father and goes along with acting the part of a wife to him, in so doing inevitably despising her mother. But unconsciously she is oppressed by his power, acknowledges his wickedness, and wants him, as expressed in a number of the novels, dead. When the father is dead, the children are at liberty to discover who they are.'

'I don't accept that. Charlotte M. Yonge was a deeply religious Victorian woman. She could not have gone along with having sex with her father,' Katherine said.

'It probably started when she was quite young; before she knew what sex was. Also, in the nineteenth century incest was probably looked on rather differently than it is today. Susan Brownmiller writes in *Against Our Will* of a case in America at the turn of the century where the Washington

State Supreme Court refused damages to a girl who had been raped by her father on the grounds that . . .' She rummaged in her carrier bag and quoted, '"The rule of law prohibiting suits between parent and child is based on the interest that society has in preserving harmony in domestic relations." Although the law in England might not have been identical to that in America – I still have to check on that – Yonge would certainly have held the prevailing view that domestic harmony was everything! I mean, think about it. Has it never occurred to you how odd it is that Yonge made the suitor of the mother who then marries the daughter a manufacturer of umbrellas?'

'I can't say it has,' Katherine said, who had thought it odd.

'Yonge is a middle-class snob. By and large she disapproves of both the aristocracy and tradespeople with pretensions to gentility. Her characters are doctors, clergy, minor landowners and gentlemen who stay in their libraries. When Felix, in *The Pillars of the House*, is unable to go to university but has to apprentice himself to a printer to support his siblings, Yonge makes plain the awfulness of his sacrifice. He was giving up his position as a gentleman and his right to marry a gentlewoman. Yet here you have the character who marries Nutty given to trade. And what a trade! Out of her unconscious she makes him a manufacturer of umbrellas, the ultimate phallic symbol, an image redolent of sex.'

The Pearls in their individual ways thought about umbrellas.

'I don't see why an umbrella has anything to do with sex,' Maisy said.

Nobody said anything.

After a pause Georgina said, 'Closed male, open female.'

'I still don't see.'

'Penises and vulvas, you know,' Grace said. 'Shut, penis, open, vulva.'

'I think that's silly. Just silly. Anything can be interpreted that way. She might have made him a manufacturer of nuts and bolts or a flower seller,' said Annabel waving her arms.

'The interesting thing is that she made him a manufacturer at all. I cannot recall a single other case of a central character being in industry. Then she chooses him to be a maker of an explicit symbol of penetrative sex.'

They racked their brains for examples of important characters in trade.

'I agree that Miss Yonge was a snob,' Katherine said. 'But the reason why it was all right for Nutty to marry a manufacturer is because her mother was a governess. It was therefore a perfectly fitting marriage. As for her father being an aristocrat, we all know what she thought of *them*.'

'It's all nonsense,' Annabel repeated. 'Her father was a good man, best friends with Keble, and built a church.'

'Steeple,' Grace said and giggled.

'And,' Katherine continued with her argument, 'even if it were true – and I don't accept that it is – and Mr Dutton *is* an unconscious sexual symbol, I really don't see that this necessarily means that Charlotte M. Yonge was a sexually abused child.'

'You have to bring together the evidence of the complicated way Yonge treated fathers and mothers in her other fiction and add that to the curious tale of *Nutty's Father* in which the mother hands over the care of a gross and disgusting father to her only daughter. Then the daughter is saved by being penetrated by the mother's lover, whom the girl has looked upon as a substitute father. Also, there can be little doubt that Yonge despised her mother. In part this would have been because she realised that she had supplanted her as a companion, acolyte and ultimately – I believe – as a wife to her father. In her fiction mothers are either negligible, vegetable or dead.'

'Absurd,' Maisy said.

'Even when she tackles a good father – Dr May, in *The Daisy Chain* – she has him kill his wife and cripple his eldest daughter. And then she sacrifices Ethel, the heroine, to father worship. Everybody has blamed Christabel Coleridge for destroying Yonge's papers after she finished writing her life. Given the times, she might well have had good reason to do so. They probably divulged too much of Yonge's relationships with both her father and Keble.'

'Keble!' shrieked Maisy, Georgina and Moira together.

'I think it might be difficult to prove they had an affair, but it is hard to ignore the amount of good men attached to good but enfeebled women in her novels. She was fixated with the situation and it cannot be an accident that Keble's wife was an invalid.'

'Very far-fetched,' Katherine said. 'I agree she had a thing about crippled women and they are always portrayed as fine examples of womanhood, but that almost certainly had to do with her friend Marion Dyson who, like the most notable cripple in her fiction, Cherry in *The Pillars of the House*, was married to no one.'

'I agree Yonge's peculiar friendship with Marion Dyson needs to be fully explored,' Hilary said recklessly. She had not intended to embark on this question as she was still feeling her way to an understanding of Yonge's and Dyson's relationship. Probably it would come to nothing. She had more hopes of

Keble who had stepped so easily after her father's death into his shoes, and at the foot of whose memorial in the churchyard at Otterbourne Yonge had been buried.

Reeling with shock on Hilary's departure the Pearls sat in silence looking at the floor.

'She has a publisher?' Annabel asked, host-like, breaking the silence.

'Yes,' Moira said.

Grace said, 'There seemed to be an awful lot of accusations; it's difficult to remember them all.'

'We should make a list of them.' Katherine tried to inject some energy into her voice. 'Grace, take down what we say.'

Moira, 'Incest with her father.'

Maisy, 'Adultery with Keble.'

Georgina, 'A lesbian relationship with Marion Dyson.'

'She didn't quite say that,' said Portia, objecting to the lesbian suggestion.

'She came very close,' Katherine said. 'Then there was all that nonsense about Charlotte M. Yonge despising mothers. She simply does not understand in the least what character traits Miss Yonge found admirable in women.'

They lapsed into silence again, exhausted. Their old bones sank heavily into the cushions of their chairs. Katherine felt as though her brain were pickled in ether.

'Laura should be here,' Maisy said, slightly slurring her speech.

At that moment the front doorbell rang.

'Laura!' said Annabel brightly, wishing everyone gone.

It was indeed Laura. For once Maisy was pleased to see

her. The others used Maisy's departure to leave without attempting to discuss matters further.

Annabel lapsed into a light coma after they left. Jane, the nurse, judged that the occasion had been too much for her and must not happen again.

Chapter Seven

'You do realise that you can't go back to Saint-Barthélemy yet,' Katherine said on the telephone to Moira the day after the meeting around Annabel's bedside.

'No, I don't. I'm going on Thursday.' It was Tuesday.

'You can't possibly go. We have to decide what to do about Hilary Greep.'

'I'm going on Thursday. There is nothing we can do about Hilary Greep. She's a happening. A geological fault. An act of God. A nuclear what-not.'

'She is nothing of the kind. She is a silly little girl and has to be put a stop to.'

'I'm going. I've got things to do.'

'You and I are the only Pearls who are both mentally and physically able. You have to stay and help put a stop to this travesty of truth.'

'You can use Grace to trot around and do errands. And why not make Portia stay around and help. Somerset is much more accessible than Saint-Barthélemy. Staying away from one's home in the West Indies is much more of a thing than not taking the train down to Somerset.'

'She has Alzheimer to look after.'

If Katherine had been talking to Maisy, Maisy would have snorted with laughter. Moira was cross. 'That's an unkind way to talk. I'm not prepared to hang around London at your whim. There is nothing we can do to save Charlotte . . .' damn, she'd said it, 'from Hilary Greep's bad faith. In fact, I'm fed up with it all. I want my sunshine, my blossoms, my cat, my comfortable bed and my sundowner. I'm not sure we shouldn't disband the Pearls. Most of us are dead, some of us are half dead, the rest of us soon will be dead, and the present generation thinks Charlotte M. Yonge is a floor plan.'

She put down the telephone. She did have things to do. She must return to Saint-Barthélemy and reorganise her papers. Since listening to Hilary Greep she had decided that she must let Auden off the hook. No hanky-panky in the corridor of his apartment. No historical revision. He could lie blissful in his heavenly bed as little pink cherubs wee-weed champagne into his mouth. Or whatever. Such a pity! She sighed. Of course she was upset about Charlotte. Very upset. With clumsy fingers she fished her small address book out of her handbag and looked up the number of her travel agent. Quick, she thought, before Katherine got her.

The telephone rang. She let it ring and ring. She walked round her sitting-room as it rang. She went to the lavatory. That took time. Her bowel movement wasn't what it was. She rather liked sitting on the lavatory as the phone rang. It relaxed her. It wasn't like being in the sitting-room with it. There it became an alien pet, holding her at bay as it growled and spat, demanding the attention she did not intend to give. Katherine was a bully. No wonder Kenneth had been so unfaithful to her. She wondered for the umpteenth time if Katherine had known. He had certainly had Percy and Georgina, and others. Marriage. Goodness, she'd been lucky.

All that emotional pain, cooking and physical squalor, food particles and bad nights. Snoring. She could snore blissfully in peace and present her romantic surfaces to the public.

The telephone stopped ringing. She went to the bedroom and examined herself in the mirror. She smoothed away her double chin and saw herself in a wimple with the high white starch of the habit cutting off her double chin from view. Perhaps she should have been an adventurous nun! Nuns could do most things nowadays. Probably even sit on a sunlit terrace with a sundowner.

She was on the telephone to her travel agent when the doorbell rang.

Katherine was on the doorstep.

'You are *not* welcome,' Moira shrieked down the intercom, but she let her in.

As the lift cranked its way up the well to her landing, she had a momentary wish that it would drop. Only if it did, she would probably have a heart attack and never get out to Saint-Barthélemy.

'Coffee?' she asked as she showed Katherine into her small, featureless sitting-room.

'It's nearly twelve. Why don't you let me take you out to lunch?' Katherine suggested in her most amiable manner.

Moira was swayed. 'It won't change my mind, you know.'

'No? Well, even if it doesn't we would have a jollier time discussing it over lunch and a bottle of wine.'

'I know a nice place.' Moira was warming to the idea. 'Quite small and within walking distance. Teddy introduced me to it quite recently. I paid, of course.'

'I'm not sure that I would be prepared to be seen in public with Teddy any more. He steals my books and has a dirty, unbuttoned look about him.'

'And smelly. I was sure his chair cushion would smell when we left. Not very nice for the next person sitting down to have a meal. But what can you do? I could hardly have him here, polluting the furniture. Next time, I will take him somewhere with plastic seating.'

'Percy is supposed to clean for him once a week. She must be slacking.' Katherine made a note in her diary. 'Let's go.'

'She needs to wash his clothes,' Moira said, gathering up her things. 'But it's also a question of personal hygiene. I expect he's given up bathing. She can hardly help him with that.' Moira knew the difficulty of bathing. Nowadays she had to turn on all fours to get out of the bath. It was all right in Saint-Barthélemy. There she showered. But no bathroom in London had ever had such a thing. Sometimes she stood in the bath and hosed herself down with the hair-shower attachment. She wondered if Teddy had such a thing on his bath. If so, he should be encouraged to use it.

'I don't see why she shouldn't help him bath. It's not as though there is anything he has that she hasn't seen before.'

'You seem to forget that Percy is as old as he is. He's not skinny. I doubt she could shift him.'

'I forget nothing.' Katherine sometimes thought Percy should be punished for a lifetime of self-indulgent delinquency.

They lunched well (Moira particularly so) and talked about the personalities of Katherine's pekes. Moira knew she was going to stay and so it was only as she was finishing her profiteroles that she enquired, 'Well, what are we going to do about Hilary Greep?'

'First, find out a great deal more about her. What is her academic background? How far advanced is she with the

87

book? Has she received any money up front? How many copies does she keep of her work? Does she work on a word processor? Does she live alone, with other girls, or a boyfriend? Is the boyfriend get-at-able? Who is her supervisor? Illnesses? Mental stability? Background? Would she be seducible with a grand job offer? You know.'

'Some of those options sound as though you are thinking of stealing her work.'

'I don't think we should rule out anything.'

Moira felt a *frisson* of excitement tingle down her back.

'I think you should continue to befriend her. Try to break through all that sentimental guff about sisterhood and find out what her origins really are. I'll make enquiries about her academic credentials at Birkbeck College. Once we have found out a bit more, we'll consult with the others.'

'I wish the weather were nicer,' Moira sighed as she heaved herself up. 'I wouldn't mind staying on here so much if it were.'

'It will probably improve, now that April's here,' Katherine consoled her, leaving a carefully calculated, adequate tip on the table.

Portia was relieved to be back in the West Country. It was surprising how upset she felt about the distortions being foisted upon Charlotte M. Yonge's life. What right had Hilary Greep to use her to aid her doctrinaire ambitions? It would be infinitely better were Charlotte M. Yonge's books to moulder into dust on the shelves of second-hand book shops and her name forgotten except for the weathered markings on her gravestone in Otterbourne, than for her to be put under Hilary Greep's merciless, unfriendly spotlight. She would have hated it so. You live, you die. Your reputation is the shadowy reality between birth and death. Nothing else adheres except those marks you make during that time. Then along comes Hilary Greep who shines her torch on you, and then plays shadow puppets with her fingers in the reflected light. Everybody knows that shadows cast against the light are distortions.

So thought Portia as she baked bread and cakes and boiled Archie and her son Harry's shirts in a big tub on the solid-fuel Aga. Nowadays she could no longer lift the scuttle high enough to pour in the coke, so Terry the garden boy did it when he came into work at eight-thirty in the morning. She worked with great vigour, trying to obliterate the four days of her absence. She wished to get the shirts out of the way before Friday when Anna was coming down with three or four friends. One of her other daughters, Mary, and her two children, Portia's granddaughters, were also coming for the school holidays. They always made a silly fuss because Harry brought his dirty washing home from London. Portia liked to do things for Harry. She felt that if she worked hard enough at making him feel that he was the master they could both forget that she still held the reins of the property in her hands. She had no desire to become a pensioner on the land. It would be time enough to think, and maybe only think, of handing over once he was married. With children.

Although Portia's children encouraged their friends to exclaim at the boiling tub on the stove she always carried on regardless; men could not be expected to wash clothes and boiling was so much better for shirts than those cool washes of professional laundries. Anyway, nowadays Archie's under-clothes needed boiling. She preferred, however, not to run the gauntlet of their jokes unnecessarily.

At eleven-thirty Mr Baxter stalked in. Without glancing at

her or saying 'Good morning' he filled the Aga. Portia's heart sank. It meant there was trouble with Terry. She allowed him to leave, pretending to be too preoccupied to notice his mood. She would sort it out in the afternoon.

She was putting the bread in the oven when Mrs Willis came into the kitchen with Archie. Their linked hands fell apart.

'You're back,' said Mrs Willis cheerfully. She was a plump woman in her middle sixties with tightly permed grey hair and thick legs.

'No!' said Archie.

Portia did not attempt to kiss Archie; she could see he would push her aside. 'Yes. How has it been?' she asked Mrs Willis.

'Fine. We've been fine, haven't we, Mr Sheldon?'

'Let's have tea,' Portia said, knowing it was expected of her.

'Come and sit down, Mr Sheldon.' Mrs Willis pulled out a chair and patted Archie into it. Pulling out another chair, she sat down beside him. As she talked, she now and again patted him on his knee. Archie was calm and undemanding.

'We've just been for a walk, haven't we, Mr Sheldon? We picked some primroses, didn't we? But we dropped them, didn't we, when we were patting the horses?'

'Yes.' Archie beamed around him.

Just for a moment Portia wanted to slap Mrs Willis. Instead, she put her arm around Archie's shoulders and said, 'Cake, Mrs Willis?'

Mrs Willis took a slice and put it on Archie's plate. 'There!' she said.

Archie said, 'Thank you,' and, seemingly oblivious to Portia's arm draped round his neck, started eating.

'Lovely manners, Mr Sheldon has, hasn't he?' Mrs Willis

90

said. She added, 'Delicious,' appreciatively as she took another slice for herself.

'There weren't any problems in the village?'

'No. You never escaped me for a minute, did you, Mr Sheldon?' She winked at him. 'But we had a fine old time, didn't we?'

Archie smiled.

Portia sat down across the table from them. She thought Archie's smile was sly. I should be grateful to her, she thought. Archie is happy with her. I should go away more often, but I won't. I won't leave her with him again.

'Mr Baxter came in yesterday. He says Terry hasn't turned up for work since you've been away.'

'Oh dear! He is naughty! I'll ring the hostel and find out what has happened.'

'What's happened is he hit a boy of thirteen.'

'Oh dear. I expect he was provoked. His temper can be a little uncertain but there is always a reason for it.'

'I don't know about that, but I expect he'll have to go back to the institution.'

'I doubt it. There isn't any room for people like Terry there now, thank goodness.'

'I don't think Mr Baxter likes working with someone that unpredictable.'

'Mr Baxter has worked with Terry for many years and knows how to manage him.'

'He said he was useless.'

'Ah! That's another matter.'

As she cleared the table, Portia reviewed her options over Terry. It would mean wading through the bureaucracy of meetings with his social worker. Finding out what really happened. Talking to the hostel. The last time this had happened it had taken weeks to sort out. His offence had been talking to a twelve-year-old girl at the swimming baths at Butlin's in Minehead. Portia appreciated the underlying sexuality of Terry's behaviour, but she considered there was a general failure to understand that people like Terry often felt socially more comfortable with children than adults. The outcome was that Terry was so thoroughly frightened by being questioned by the police he had never gone swimming again. The social workers had also insisted that he live in a hostel rather than at the manor. They said because she often had grandchildren staying it was better he should not live in.

She rang the hostel.

John and Laura met in a restaurant for lunch near his office in Soho Square. It was crowded and the tables were set closely together. John hoped that the lack of privacy would prevent Laura's indulgence in histrionics. The lunch was to be his last effort to work out an accommodation with her about what should happen to their mother. He had a feeling that Laura was being nicer to her at the moment.

'Wouldn't you be lonely on your own?' he asked her. 'What about if we had someone come in to help four hours a day?'

'I probably *will* be lonely and feel guilty on my own,' Laura replied crossly. 'But there are different ways of being lonely. Being with someone you do not wish to be with is far more lonely than being on one's own. Anyway, there are worse things in life than loneliness and it is possible that Mummy is learning about one of them now – dependency! Perhaps I am teaching Mummy about dependency.' She looked down demurely, cut a bit of steak, piled it with spinach on her fork and popped it in her mouth.

How disgusting people look as they eat, John thought. 'So you are teaching her a lesson in dependency by not getting her up at a regular time in the morning?'

'Life,' Laura explained, 'is a journey on which the traveller acquires knowledge, and nobody is too old to learn. I suppose it is possible that this is the reason I am occasionally unkind to her.' She found she was also learning more about herself by looking after her mother. She liked watching the base nature, which she had previously ignored, flower. She had to find amusement somewhere in her stark situation.

'I think Mummy is very lucky. If she were the widow of an Indian peasant she would probably have been burnt alive. She should count her blessings rather than complain to you.'

'You don't even give her telephone messages.'

'That's ridiculous. She has a telephone by her bed and in the sitting-room.' She started looking at the pudding menu. 'I want out. If things go on, I shall probably end up being a horrible person, which would be a pity because I think I probably do love her a bit.'

The following Sunday Maisy had lunch with John and Maureen.

'Would you prefer to go into a home?' John asked. 'There really are some very nice ones. You would be entirely independent, coming and going. If you really objected to eating in the communal dining-room you could always have take-aways brought in to you. You could have your books and everything. It would just mean that there would be somebody on call when you wanted to go to the lavatory or for bathing, and they would help you get up in the morning and go to bed.'

'No,' Maisy said passionately. 'Why should I?'

It was the end of the meal. They were eating chocolate mousse in individual cartons from Marks & Spencer. John and Maureen's son, Maurice, down from Leicester University, had left them because he did not believe in eating dairy products. The dining-room/kitchen was in the basement of their West Kensington terraced house. Getting Maisy down there was an haphazard affair. A few years earlier John had found a light Edwardian wicker day-bed with carrying handles at either end, and in this he would transfer Maisy from the car to the house. After a 'before-lunch drink' in the sitting-room he and Maureen would again stagger, since the internal staircase was steeper and more awkwardly angled than the outside one, back out of the house and down the basement steps to the kitchen. Neighbourhood children often attended their passage shouting encouragement and advice. John, Maureen and Maisy did not enjoy the theatre they provided.

'I've got a perfectly suitable flat all my own, and I have lived in it for forty years. My wheelchair can go anywhere in it. There are only four functions I find difficult to do for myself. Cooking, dressing, undressing and going to the bathroom. Many people live at home with greater difficulties.'

'It's impossible not to notice that you and Laura seem to rub each other up the wrong way. Some people are just not suited to nursing and Laura is one of them. If you were to go into protected housing outside central London your flat plus your annuity, coupled with some topping up from us, would do the trick. In fact we've found an excellent place with a pretty garden in South Acton. The alternative would be live-in agency nurses who change over every fortnight, a housekeeper, or live-in couple. The latter rarely work well long-term and both those options are more expensive than the home. I don't think we can afford them.'

Such despair filled Maisy that she was unsure of her voice. Powerlessness. 'I won't be put away.'

John rose clumsily to his feet, and rushing round the table pulled a chair out next to her. Sitting so close that the chair legs touched he took her hands. 'We have to discuss it. Things can't go on as they are. Laura isn't nice to you.'

'I won't.' Maisy's strangled voice was fierce. 'Laura isn't suited to nursing,' she mimicked. 'What is Laura suited to? You could say that she gladdened your father's eye, but he's not here now. She certainly doesn't gladden any other man's eye! She's fifty years old . . .'

'Forty-nine,' John corrected.

'And has nothing to show for it. Charlotte M. Yonge looked after her sick mother until she died. She didn't enjoy it; why should she? But despite being an artist and incidentally the most popular novelist in England she did her duty, not gladly but not badly. She did not make her mother's life a misery because she would prefer to footle around doing something else like Laura.'

'You're being cruel, Mummy. Nobody's life is wasted unless they feel it is. Laura did not feel her life was wasted when she was Peter Coggins's secretary at the Commons. She enjoyed being there and working for him.'

'He was a completely mediocre man with dandruff who spent his time asking asinine questions in Parliament on behalf of the trucking industry. The rest of the time he spent lunching.'

'That's not the point.'

95

'I wish I believed in God. Laura would not go to heaven.' Maisy withdrew her hands from under John's. He was making her feel pathetic. 'Disgusting little Conservative,' she added.

'Who?' John asked lightly, going back to his chair. 'Peter Coggins or Laura?'

'Both.'

Maisy was a snob. She was not conscious of it because she had embraced the Labour Party on meeting her husband, David Armstrong, in 1940. Before the war she had driven an ambulance for the Red Cross in Spain on the Nationalist side and had written poetry which had received some critical attention. She had been lucky in having a governess who had instilled in her a love of literature and of political philosophy, to the bemusement of her horse-loving parents. Her life until she broke loose in Spain had been that of the ageing débutante: parties, night-clubs, house-parties, concerts and galleries. Having been on the wrong side in the Spanish Civil War did her no harm with David. They met in Hampstead at a party given by a journalist, an old acquaintance from Spain. David was the handsomest man she had ever seen; almost pretty, with blond hair, a fresh complexion and curly lips which broke into the sweetest smile. There is nothing more enjoyable than successfully converting a bright, pretty girl to the error of her ways and so David in his turn fell in love with Maisy. At the advanced age of thirty-one he was in the army, on leave from Balliol. After the war he decided not to return to Balliol, and instead they settled in Hampstead in the flat Maisy still called 'home'. Maisy fell passionately in love with bookish, middle-class bohemian life.

They were never quite rich enough to have regular help. Having been brought up by nannies, Maisy found the constant presence of children an unnatural intrusion, while their illnesses filled her with a debilitating anxiety. Once they were launched into adulthood and she had the flat and David to herself, her pleasure in their life together was almost unbounded and remained unbroken. After his untimely death ten years ago from pneumonia at the age of seventy-six, Maisy had embraced her loneliness with a violence that excluded her family. Friends she could tolerate better. By now she had filed her loneliness away in a box so that she was hardly conscious of it. Suddenly, with the prospect of being bundled away to Acton, she was utterly bereft. She would *not* be humiliated in front of her friends. The round table; the strange son; the horrible basement in which she found herself; all were alien territory. Inwardly she saw her parents' drawing-room: a high, long, sunlit room filled with an all-over russet glow given by polished wood, silver, and the heavy green-gold curtains masking french windows on to lawn. She could smell the damp spaniels and hear the sucking noises they made as they licked themselves. What was she doing here? How could her life have led to this mean house, and these unkind people?

'Will you look at it? We could drive out there this afternoon,' John suggested.

'No,' Maisy said.

'It's very odd,' Katherine said to Moira on the telephone. 'Nobody has heard of her. She isn't registered at Birkbeck College. I think she's a fake.'

'She's being very elusive. I've tried asking her to lunch, tea, cocktails and dinner. I fear she is avoiding me. I've got her telephone number but when I tried to check her address in the telephone book, nobody is registered under the name Greep.

I also tried ringing Telecom in case it was a new number but it isn't.'

'Perhaps she's a fantasist and not writing anything. She could be a mental patient doing a project on Charlotte M. Yonge as therapy.'

'When I first met her in the London Library, there was a moment when I wondered if she had changed her name. But then I thought, who would change their name to Greep, and dismissed the idea.'

'What gave you the idea that she might have changed her name?'

'It's difficult to remember exactly. She asked me if I had changed my name and there was something about the way she asked that made me think, for a moment, that she had changed hers. How would we go about finding out?'

There was silence while they both thought.

'We can hardly advertise for anyone who knows the antecedents of Hilary Greep to get in touch. She might see it,' Moira said.

'Since she obviously registered under her real name when she went up to Birkbeck College, the change to Hilary Greep must be fairly recent – not more than a year or two. It's possible she joined the London Library under her original name. She probably joined even before she was accepted for a postgraduate degree at Birkbeck.'

'Even if she joined under her baptismal name, I can't see how it helps. How do you find out what it is?'

'I'll find out,' Katherine said. 'I have a cosy relationship with one of the library assistants.'

And she did.

'Dear Portia,' she wrote on a card, 'Hilary Greep's baptismal name is Cherry Blossom. Love, Katherine.'

'Dear Georgina,' she wrote, 'Hilary Greep's real name is Cherry Blossom. Love, Katherine.'

'Dear Maisy,' she wrote, 'Hilary Greep's real name is Cherry Blossom. Love, K.'

'Darling Annabel,' she wrote. 'I hope you have recovered from hosting the Pearls' meeting last week. I have discovered that Hilary Greep is really called Cherry Blossom. Ha ha. I would love to come and have tea next Tuesday if that is agreeable to you. Love, Katherine.'

Dear Grace,

The girl masquerading as a biographer of Charlotte M. Yonge is really called Cherry Blossom. She lives at 303 Loftus Road in Shepherd's Bush. She is avoiding Moira so please could you go round and invite her to tea or some other meal. At the meal find out 1) How far advanced she is with the book. 2) How many copies she has. 3) Is it written on computer. 4) Does she have back-up on floppy disks. 5) Has she got a boyfriend and if so what is he called and what does he do. 6) Does she live with anyone else. 7) Where in England do her parents live. 8) What are her vices and pleasures.

I am sorry to ask you to do this but I think it more likely she will talk to you than to me. Once we have this information I think we should probably all meet again. K.

Grace was very angry. She rang up Georgina. 'Who does she think she is?' she asked.

'I think at the moment she probably thinks she is a general with some pretty hopeless soldiers at her command. General

Patten was supposed to have said of his troops, "They're like a bunch of bananas, some green, some yeller and some plain rotten." I don't know what she and Moira are up to, but they obviously think you are part of the able-bodied brigade. You *could* look on the letter as a compliment.'

'I don't. If she's a general she's seeing me as a foot soldier.'

'Well, darling, you *are* still pretty nimble. And your legs have kept their shape. No knobbly bits like me.'

'I'm going to refuse. How can I go out to Shepherd's Bush and knock on that strange girl's door? She probably wouldn't recognise me.'

'They kill each other a lot in Shepherd's Bush. Georgio tells me there are mounds of flowers on every street corner. Very ghoulish habit, I think.'

'You mean it's no place even for a sprightly old lady like myself?' Grace put down the telephone feeling a lot more cheerful.

Katherine rang Moira. 'I've had a very rum card from Grace. It says, "Can't go. They kill old ladies in Shepherd's Bush."'

'Ring her up,' Moira advised. 'She's never able to say no when tackled directly. But be nice to her.'

Katherine was. And Grace capitulated.

Chapter Eight

And that's another thing, Grace thought to herself as she went up the stairs in Georgina's house, I must ask Georgina how I am to get rid of Percy. She was reminded about the difficulty of Percy because Percy had opened the door to her, and Grace had found herself unable to say anything but, 'How are you?' and, 'How is your lumbago?' To which Percy had replied, 'Not too bad at the moment, thank you,' adding, 'You'll find Mrs Matheson in the upstairs sitting-room.' Percy had been wearing bedroom slippers. It was the slippers that had finally made Grace attempt to dismiss her. It was bad enough that she wore furry slippers as she cleaned the house, but then Grace had found them neatly laid beside the bed in the spare bedroom and she knew it was only a matter of time before Percy started sleeping over. After all, she did it all the time at Georgina's and at that ghastly poet Teddy Linklater's flat, and she had even been known to sleep on Katherine's sofa. Did she have nowhere of her own to go?

'Doesn't Percy have anywhere of her own to sleep?' she asked Georgina as she kissed her.

'I don't know. She's never mentioned it if she has. For all one knows she has a cottage with roses climbing round

the front door in Surbiton. I'll get her to make some tea.'
Georgina went out on to the landing and called down the
stairs, 'Percy, Percy, could we have some tea, please.'

'Down here, in the drawing-room,' Percy screeched back
from the hall.

'She's left her slippers by the spare bed. It's the last straw.
I don't want her working for me. She comes in when it suits
her and sometimes doesn't come at all. And she's always
putting chairs and cushions at angles. And no amount of
telling her that I like things straight makes any difference.
She swapped two small incidental tables around the other
day. And she whistles or rather hoots as she works.'

'I haven't heard that. Why don't you just tell her you don't
want her any more?'

'I've tried that. Last week she was complaining about her
lumbago and I said I thought the work was too much for
her and that she shouldn't come any more. I gave her an
extra ten pounds at the end of the day and said it was a
farewell present. But I know she's been in this week while I
was out seeing Robert. She'd used the bath and all the chairs
had been put in the wrong places again. Why do you put up
with her?'

'I don't really know. Percy has always considered that
I owed her a job. I inherited her as part of my husband's
chattels. She was there when I got back from honeymoon,
and since I was always in bed, God knows what went on.
I have always said that she could not live in, but she never
took me seriously. Let's go down and have tea; Percy can't
manage the stairs with the tray any longer.'

As they went slowly down the doorbell rang.

Georgina yelled at Percy who was on her way to answer it,
'Keep the chain on, and if it's Rentokil, don't let them in.'

'It is,' Percy shouted back and pushed the door shut.

The bell rang again.

Georgina limped to the door and opened it the crack allowed by the chain.

'Mr Matheson sent us, ma'am. He said you knew about it. We've just come to check the house for dry rot. We won't be doing any work. Mr Matheson would just like a report.'

'Well, you can't come now. It's not convenient.'

Georgina closed the door.

The tea and jaffa cakes, left on the tray, were waiting for them in the drawing-room.

Georgina poured.

'Don't you mind her staying the night?' Grace asked, continuing with her grievance.

'Not really. The house is big enough and it's not as though she uses anything up. I'm hardly aware when she stays and when she doesn't. It can be quite useful. She puts on my electric blanket before I go to bed. Don't you find you're always cold nowadays?'

'No. I don't think so,' Grace said doubtfully.

'Georgio is always complaining, and he's younger than us. Any change in Robert?'

'No. Not really, but I'm sure, sometimes, that he recognises me.'

Georgina leant forward. 'Oh! How does he show it?' She was really interested.

'It's just a feeling I have.' That morning when Grace had raised the sheet covering Robert's tummy his penis was raised at half-mast to greet her. It was like receiving a love letter. She was still overflowing with love for him. 'I'm thinking of bringing him back home; that would stop Percy sleeping over.'

Georgina changed the subject. 'Did you see Hilary Greep
– or Cherry Blossom, as I like to think of her?'

'Yes.'

'Tell.'

'I went there yesterday afternoon. I rang up first to make
sure she was in and put down the receiver when she answered.
Then I drove out to Shepherd's Bush. Have you ever been
there? It takes hours.'

'I suppose I have in my time.'

'The traffic is terrible. I thought she might well have gone
out by the time I got there, and then it was difficult to park.
I couldn't help remembering what you told me about crime
in Shepherd's Bush, so I left my handbag at home, and took
just enough money to get a taxi in case a crisis arose, and I
was careful not to wear any jewellery, like when you walk
around Naples.'

'Get on,' Georgina said impatiently.

'I must say I didn't want to ring her bell. It was so
embarrassing to force myself on a stranger like that. Also
I hadn't liked her.'

'Go on.'

'She was in. She had one of those speaker things that flats
have. I tried to explain that I was a Pearl and that I just
happened to be passing and I thought it would be nice to
take her out to tea if she knew a place in Shepherd's Bush
we could go to. I don't really think she understood what I
was saying, but she buzzed me in and came running down
the stairs without any shoes on. Then I explained all over
again, and she said she didn't have any shoes on so perhaps
I should come upstairs. I don't know what she thought. I
felt an awful fool.

'You should see her flat! It's one room and squalid. She

had obviously been in bed, which was just a mattress on the floor, covered in books, and a plate with some dried-out-looking baked beans on it. I don't think she changes the sheets very often. They were that bluey grey that things become if you mix coloureds in with your white wash. My maid once did it to all my underwear and I had to go out and buy everything new.

'She said she didn't really know where there was a place suitable to go to for tea, and she didn't as a rule have tea at tea time, but she would be very happy to make tea if I didn't mind the squalor. She did actually say that! I said that I would love to have a cup of tea although, actually, if the truth be told, I did rather mind the squalor. There was nowhere to sit. In the end I sat on her desk chair and she rolled up the bed with all sorts of things still in it, and sat on the rolled-up roll. So I was sort of talking down to her. She gave me a mug with a tea bag in it.'

'Any biscuits?' asked Georgina, taking one herself.

'No.'

'Go on.'

'I said how fascinated I had been by her talk on Charlotte M. Yonge, and that it had given me much food for thought, and that I wondered how far advanced she was with her book because I so much looked forward to reading it.'

'Well?'

'She's halfway through it.'

'How long until she finishes?'

'Nine months.'

They were silent as they thought about this.

'I can't see what Katherine thinks we can do about it,' Georgina said.

'Then I asked if she had a publisher, as I was sure Moira could help if she hadn't.'

'Has she?'

'Yes. Halifax University Press.'

'Halifax!'

'I didn't know Halifax had a university or a press.'

'Neither did I. The book might just die a natural dim death, killed off by its publisher.'

'Only she says she may be transferring to Chatto. She said she had met somebody from there at a party who showed considerable interest when she explained what she was doing, and suggested that she should send the book to her.'

'What else did she say?'

'Well, I didn't ask about boyfriends because we know she's celibate. She said so at the meeting. It was obvious that she worked on a computer because there was one on her desk. So I showed a great deal of interest in that, saying I had always thought I was too old to master such magical technology but I knew people who had. I asked her if she kept copies on floppy disk as she must be so nervous, living in such an area, that her computer might be stolen. I said it had happened to a friend and that he had gone into a decline.'

'I'm not sure you should have said that. Now, if Katherine decides to steal it, you will be an obvious suspect.'

'She wouldn't do that, would she?' Grace was shocked. 'Anyway, people don't suspect old women of stealing.'

'What about the Baroness de Stemple; she's an example to us all.'

'She was a wicked woman.'

'No. She was a delinquent woman. If Katherine were to steal Miss Greep's computer, would you say that would make her wicked or delinquent? And would you say that Katherine had become wicked or delinquent quite suddenly? Or would you think she has always been all of those things, but that they had never emerged until she was overwhelmed by the temptation to steal Miss Greep's computer?'

'This is a silly conversation. Katherine sits on committees judging moral issues all the time.'

'Just a thought. Have you told her about your visit to Hilary Greep yet?'

'No. I thought I'd keep her waiting. Anyway, it wouldn't do her any good to steal the computer. Hilary says that she is completely, phobicly neurotic about the possibility of having her computer and disks stolen, so she always makes three copies, one of which she carries around with her. A burglar would not only have to steal the computer and the other floppy disks, but on the same day Hilary would have to be mugged. I can't see Katherine mugging her!'

They both laughed.

'Have you noticed that Grace is behaving very rumly?' Katherine asked Moira.

They were in a taxi on the way to Annabel's for an afternoon visit. Moira had picked up Katherine on the way. Katherine was accompanied by her Pekinese, Mozart. She had decided that it would be nice for Annabel to be in touch with nature. Dying people must get tired of flowers, she thought. Mozart, snuffling on her lap, could represent the beasts of the wild. He liked outings away from the others. Katherine played with his ears. He had the most lavish ears of all her dogs.

'No. I don't think so. Why? Do you think she's going gaga?'

'Perhaps it's that. Senile dementia. If she has to be put away, I don't think I'll visit her. My days seem to be spent in an endless slog round friends who have half fallen off their perches. If anything happens to you out in Saint-Barthélemy, don't expect a visit. You will hear from me through Interflora, and that will be that.'

'If anything happens to me, the last thing I will want to think about is having anyone to stay. Why do you think Grace is going batty?'

'On your suggestion I asked her to see Cherry Blossom and find out a few things. I happen to know she accomplished her mission rather well, but she hasn't reported back. Instead she seems to have been ringing up all the Pearls and telling them about her visit while being rude about me. Odd, don't you think?'

'Not really. You aren't very nice to her.'

'Has she rung you?'

'Yes.'

'And did she say nasty things about me?'

'Actually, she didn't mention you.'

'Oh.'

'If Grace is going a bit funny I think it's because she's become mad with loneliness and sorrow since Robert's stroke.'

'Do you think so? You think beneath the goose there is a well of sensibility? I thought she only had her cheek-bones to get by on.'

'Poor Grace. She's the nearest thing among the Pearls to a Charlotte M. Yonge character. She's one of those soft, nervous widows who always relied on their husband's presence to give order to their day.'

'Mrs Curtis in *The Clever Woman of the Family*!'

'Exactly!'

'Mrs Underwood in *The Pillars of the House*!'

'Hardly! She fell downstairs on her husband's death and took to a sofa in a near vegetable condition.'

'Exactly! If one didn't jiggle Grace up she would be just like Mrs Underwood.'

'So you see yourself as "The Unrest Cure"?'

Sounding suddenly in the dumps, Katherine said, 'It's better than seizing up. Don't you sometimes feel depressed at the way your flesh has withered into petrified muscles and ligaments? No. Don't tell me!' she added, covering her ears as Moira opened her mouth, 'I don't want to know. Have you been to see Blanche since you've been back?'

'Yes. I took her a bunch of flowers. She was surrounded by them. Her children call in every week and replenish them. She could be lying on a bier. I won't go again.'

'Will you come back for her funeral?'

'No, I don't think so.'

'You can skip mine if you want.' Katherine was cheerful again.

'I will take it in bad part if you don't come to mine. It's important for grieving friends to say farewell. If there is no God we only exist in the memory of others. That, after all, is why we are pursuing Cherry Blossom or Ms Greep – in the hope that we can stop her from distorting the memory of Miss Yonge.'

'*I'm* pursuing her because she is a wilful liar. Over millions of years man painfully reached a level of sophistication that enabled him to make marks that formed a script so that the truth about peoples and events could be handed on from generation to generation. We rely on that truth to know ourselves. What we do, say, and record for posterity is what we are. And then in the late twentieth century Miss Blossom comes along and decides to murder Miss Yonge's life and works. She shan't do it!'

'Murder's a bit strong. Charlotte M. Yonge did live out her life experiencing all the pleasure and miseries that are our lot, without any interference from Cherry Blossom. For all we know, Cherry Blossom might be the merest blip on God's computer screen.'

Katherine leaned forward, dislodging Mozart who fell to the floor with a thud and lay there startled and wheezing. Just in time she restrained herself from waving a finger in front of Moira's face. 'If you get a blip on your computer screen, what do you do? You get rid of it before it becomes a confounded nuisance. The same with Cherry Blossom. I have discovered that her parents live in Welwyn Garden City. I think it's time we found out how and why Cherry Blossom became Hilary Greep.'

'If you are using the word "we" meaning you and me, the answer is no.'

'I thought we might hire a car and stop off at a good place for lunch. I don't know if you've noticed, but the weather has become rather nice. It will be fun looking at the countryside as it rolls by.'

'It will be a long day. I rather like a nap in the afternoon,' Moira said weakly.

Chapter Nine

On a glorious morning at 6.30 a.m. on the 1st of May, somewhere in the middle of the Himalayas, Annabel Bennet aged eighty-two was having breakfast in the company of her friends Gloria and Peter Tottersham, Maria Linklater and her godson Geoffrey Cardew and Geoffrey's wife Molly, when she pitched forward into her porridge, dead.

The 1st of May dawned clear and warm in London and the halo of the sun's magnificence encompassed Wales, Gloucestershire, Oxfordshire, and the south-west. Who cared what the day was like north of Humberside? Moira and Katherine certainly did not. At 9.30 a.m. a large car picked up Moira and then Katherine. By ten they were speeding out of London on to the Westway.

'Tumpty tum,' Moira said with satisfaction as fields, green and glowing in soft watery sunlight, passed them by.

'What *are* you on about?' asked Katherine.

'I feel like Pooh in springtime.'

'You look a little like Pooh,' Katherine said, not too acidly. Moira was dressed in flowing beige cotton. She carried a white cardigan, just in case.

'I feel I'm Pooh to your Rabbit.'
Moira quoted:

> Oh, the butterflies are flying,
> Now the winter days are dying,
> And the primroses are trying
> > To be seen.
> And the turtle-doves are cooing,
> And the woods are up and doing,
> For the violets are blue-ing
> > In the green.

'Stop it; it's disgusting. I have always hated Christopher Robin. It combines all that is whimsical and nauseating in our attitude to children.'

'"Hush hush, whisper who dares, Christopher Robin is saying his prayers." I love it. Whenever I feel really low and lonely I take myself off to bed with a bowl of cornflakes and cream and read *The House at Pooh Corner*.'

More likely she takes a bottle of whisky and a lust-in-the-dust-in-period-costume novel to bed, thought Katherine.

They arrived at Hatfield, only a few miles from Welwyn Garden City, at twelve o'clock. Katherine rang Mrs Blossom from a call box in a quaint pub called the Farmer's Arms leaving Moira sitting at a table with a gin and it. She had not as yet dismissed Cliff, their chauffeur. There was always the chance that the Blossoms might not be at home and that their journey would prove fruitless, but she thought it important the visit should seem spontaneous. She hoped the Blossoms would not get in touch with Cherry to say her friends Katherine Sackville and Moira Lockheart were calling on them. Much depended on their relationship with

112

their daughter. The less notice they had, the less likely they would be to ring their daughter – in any case, until after the event. Cherry Blossom might well have reason to start feeling paranoia – what with Grace's visit to her flat and then this.

The phone was answered. 'Hello.' The voice was light, young-sounding.

'Is that Mrs Blossom?' Katherine asked.

'Yes.'

'You don't know me. My name is Katherine Sackville. I know your daughter Cherry. She's such an engaging girl, isn't she? I wondered if my friend the writer Moira Lockheart and I could call on you this afternoon? Say, about two-thirty? We both think her a particularly talented girl and would love to discuss her career with you.' She knew it sounded very odd, and that if Mrs Blossom consented to see them she had two and a half hours to mull over the oddness before they arrived. But that would hardly alter the shape their conversation would take later on.

'Oh. Yes. Of course. Do come.' Mrs Blossom's voice sounded dismayed and startled all in one.

'How lovely! You don't know how much we look forward to meeting you. Will Mr Blossom be there?'

'No. He's working.'

'On a bank holiday! Poor you.'

'He's a salesman, you see. It's a good day for salesmen. People are at home.'

'Of course! Well, we look forward to seeing you.'

So she's the daughter of a salesman, Katherine thought. She could imagine that a salesman's daughter might be quite bright. Genetically speaking Cherry would be upwardly mobile. Her children, with luck, brighter than she. If

113

Katherine had ever had children they would probably have started genetically to descend the intelligence ladder. It was as good a reason as any other for not having them. Katherine was in no doubt that she had hit the intellectual pinnacle of her family tree.

She returned to Moira in the bar. 'Mrs Blossom will see us at two-thirty which will give us plenty of time for lunch. Drink up. The restaurant is in the old town. Cliff will drive us there. Then he can come back in time to take us to call on Mrs Blossom.'

The lunch at the Churnway Mill was delicious if a little fussily presented. Moira enjoyed it. Katherine hated it; she hated being hovered over, but since it was Moira's treat for coming, she did not show her annoyance.

Mrs Blossom lived in a modest, detached, red-brick, mock Edwardian house. It was at the end of a row of houses and, in American suburban style, not cut off from its neighbours by fencing. Instead, a strip of grass ran across the front of the houses with garden paths leading up to front doors. Mrs Blossom ushered them from a narrow entrance hall into a cream-and-white sitting-room where they sat together on a beige sofa slightly darker than Moira's dress. The curtains of the room were a plain dull red. There were no pictures on the walls. An empty blue vase stood on a small table to the left of the sofa. A round, Bakelite clock stood on the mantelpiece. Otherwise no ornaments distracted the gaze. Mrs Blossom, in a blue-and-white dress with a scooped neckline with a pattern of lilies of the valley, sat on the edge of an oversized, dark-brown armchair and leaned attentively towards them. The vestiges of Cherry's prettiness remained in her plump, putty-coloured face, although her eyes, unlike Cherry's, were an uninteresting hazel.

'Would you care for a cup of tea or coffee?' Mrs Blossom asked the strange women opposite her.

'We would love some tea,' Katherine said, although after their rich lunch nothing could have been further from the truth.

Moira, realising that they were unlikely to break the ice in such a formal setting, struggled to her feet. 'Do let us go with you. We would feel odd left here on our own since we've been together for days and days. We are on a tour of eighteenth-century churches and, unless stimulated, you know, by arches and stained-glass windows and such like, have little left to say to each other.' She laughed to show she was joking.

They followed Mrs Blossom back into the hall. This time Katherine took in the hall and the staircase straight in front of her. Pinned to the cream-coloured wall of the staircase were three flying ducks. She stopped.

'Oh, you don't see them very often any longer.'

'No,' Mrs Blossom said. 'My husband picked them up off a market stall some twenty years ago when Cherry was little. He used to like things in threes. One for him, one for me, and one for Cherry.'

Katherine suddenly realised that they were not ducks but birds, three greeny-blue flying birds probably dating from the thirties and very pretty. The dull blue of the rich glaze faded into a smoky green and they were small and delicately made. You could imagine them flying high in the air, their dull plumage almost black against the sky. Here was a difficult concept. Flying ducks were hideous and embarrassing. Flying ducks were not all right under any circumstances. Flying ducks meant something, they gave a message about the persons who displayed them on their walls.

115

But what about flying birds? Was there a subtle difference in having flying birds on your walls? Was it conceivable that around the country people were using as ornaments *beautiful flying ducks*? Were they *bravely* flying them, having recognised their beauty, or would they just as happily have flown ugly-coloured, coarsely made ducks? Would she, having discovered beautiful flying birds and ducks, pin them to the walls of her flat for the admiration of her friends as some (not herself) might a ceramic plate? Had she enough confidence in her own taste to shock her friends with them? Given that there were such things as beautiful flying ducks, might there not be beautiful garden gnomes?

'Katherine, where are you?' Moira called from the kitchen.

'I was just contemplating Mrs Blossom's beautiful garden gnomes, I mean ducks,' Katherine said, joining them.

Moira glanced askance at her. 'Look,' she said, pointing out of the window at the garden, 'what beautiful cherry trees Mrs Blossom has.'

'We put them in after we moved here. One for Cherry, one for me and one for Derek. Derek used to say they represented us as a family. Cherry loved the cherry trees when she was young.'

The garden, wider than it was long, went round the house, encircling it on three sides. It was mostly given over to grass with neat, narrow borders edging up to a wooden fence. The three spectacular cherry trees formed a semi-circle in the centre of the lawn. They were undoubtedly the focal point of the garden.

'Three flying birds and three cherry trees,' Katherine said.

'We have more threes than that.' Mrs Blossom poured

116

water into a teapot. 'Shall we have tea in the garden? It's quite warm.'

'Cherry is your only child.'

'Yes.'

'And the more precious for that!' Moira suggested.

Mrs Blossom led the way into the garden through french windows leading from the dining part of the room. She explained, 'We only had the windows put in three months ago. Cherry has never seen them.'

There was a small tiled terrace outside the windows with a round iron table and three chairs. They sat contemplating the blooming trees.

'So you haven't seen Cherry for a bit?' Moira said.

'No.'

'She's writing a book about a Victorian novelist very dear to our heart. A little group of admirers meet together now and then to discuss aspects of this writer's work. Cherry came to one of our meetings. She's a delightful girl. Very pretty. In fact she looks just like you.' Moira smiled at her warmly.

'Yes, she's very clever,' Mrs Blossom said.

'Did you call her Cherry because of the trees?' Katherine asked.

'No. It was the other way round. I was a country girl. My father was a cowman on a farm in Kent and my mother had been in service to the family as a nanny. I had never been anywhere when I met Derek. After we married we lived in Liverpool and I missed the country terribly. So when Cherry was born I wanted to call her Cherry to remind me of the countryside. Then when she was four we moved here and Derek planted the trees.'

'Well,' Katherine said, taking pleasure in the words as they tripped off her tongue, 'she's as pretty as a picture.'

'She is, isn't she?' Mrs Blossom said with anxious eagerness. 'I used to dress her so prettily when she was little. She really was as pretty as a picture. I could show you some photographs if you would be interested.'

'Yes. We'd love to see them,' they said in unison.

Mrs Blossom went to get her photograph album and Moira and Katherine sat contemplating the trees.

'I rather like it here,' Moira said. 'I like the way the trees are not in the border but plonk on the lawn.'

'Ummm,' Katherine said.

Mrs Blossom returned and, seated between them, opened the album. She quickly passed over wedding photographs until she came to a clean page across the middle of which was printed in capital letters in different colours the word 'Cherry'. Between each letter there was a yellow star. On the following page there was just one photograph, a bare baby on a white rug.

'She was just two weeks old,' Mrs Blossom said.

Katherine and Moira stared for as long as they thought they ought to at the picture. Moira said, 'I think one can see the promise of the prettiness to come, don't you?'

'Ummm,' Katherine said.

There were a couple of pages showing a bouncing pudding of a baby and then there appeared a pretty little girl with a bow in a frilly pink dress. The pretty little girl got taller, the frilly dresses changed colour, the hair got longer, and hair slides replaced the bow. At the age of fourteen she wore jeans but still smiled. At sixteen she was serious, and her hair only just covered her ears.

'It was a terrible day when she cut her hair. Her dad took on so. It's silly, I know, but it was as though her personality changed at the same time. Until then she was sweet and good and clever, really clever. I suppose it's silly to think she changed when she cut her hair but she did become more argumentative. We were proud of her when she got into Oxford. I suppose, really, it was after she went up to college that she really changed. She joined the socialists. Not that her dad didn't vote Labour till then. Not any more, though. Not since she joined those socialist feminists. I don't think I've seen her smile – really smile – since. We used to think she came back home just to scowl at us. We couldn't put a foot right. Every time Derek opened his mouth she was on him like a terrier, making out he was something terrible.'

'Did she have a boyfriend?' Katherine asked.

'I don't think so, although you can't be sure. Derek wouldn't have liked anything going on in the house. She brought down friends sometimes. They weren't very nice. They drank a lot. Derek's not a great drinker. He didn't like seeing her get drunk. They sat around in the kitchen after the pub closed drinking cans of beer and smoking.' Her eyes flickered away from Katherine and back again. 'Roll-ups, you know. Cherry said I was being silly and that everyone smoked roll-ups. It was cheaper than buying them with all that unnecessary packaging. But I couldn't see why she had to smoke anything at all. She didn't when she went up there. But as to any of them being real boyfriends, I don't think so. We haven't seen her for two years now. She sends a card on our birthdays and at Christmas but with no address.'

Moira took her hand and squeezed it.

Mrs Blossom looked suddenly as though she might cry.

Katherine said hastily, 'Children are impossible. Goodness knows why people become parents. I think all parents have something of the saint in their make-up. For the first ten years of their children's existence, parents give themselves up to ill

119

health. Children pick up disorders like dogs get fleas. Then they hand them on to their siblings and parents, causing the whole family to go around in a cycle of ill health. Then, just when the little brutes' immune systems start behaving properly, they start excreting spots and secreting hormones and that makes them unsightly and bad company. This can, in bad cases, continue until they are twenty-six. Cherry obviously missed out on the spots but has had a double dose of inconsiderate behaviour. I expect, though, she will come out of it quite soon. I speak as a retired headmistress of a girls' school. We must do all we can to encourage her. Did you know she has changed her name?'

'No.' Mrs Blossom was stunned.

'Well, she has. She is now called Hilary Greep.'

'I am sure it is only a professional name.' Moira thought Katherine was being particularly cruel to tell her.

'It isn't, you know,' Mrs Blossom said sadly. 'She's often said how she hated being called Cherry Blossom. She even wanted us to cut down the trees. If Derek knew she had changed her name he probably would cut down the middle one. He's threatened to in the past. I don't think I can tell him.'

Katherine thought of giving her Cherry's address, but decided against it. If Hilary Greep was to be neutralised by being turned back into Cherry Blossom, Mr and Mrs Blossom's overtures to their daughter would need to be carefully orchestrated. Although Mrs Blossom might be trained, Mr Blossom's responses might prove difficult to control. Instead she said, rising, 'Perhaps it will take the cutting down of the middle tree to make Cherry return to you. She lives in London, you know. We will keep in touch, give you news of her, and help in any way we can to heal the rift between you. Children who fail to come to terms with their parents do not flourish in adult life, or so I'm told.'

They left after warm farewells.

Mrs Blossom felt very odd after they had left. She felt drained and knew that she had given too much of herself to them. The mild, daily depression she had lived with since the estrangement with Cherry now took definite form, leaving her feeling malformed. It was large, dark and ugly, and in the absence of her husband, looked like him. She wished she could weep for the next forty years of her life but felt too sickened for that. Like Cherry, she wished the lawn were plain and bare. All ornamentation was a distraction to the feeling inside her.

On the way back to London Moira fell asleep in the car, the drink, good lunch and emotional conversation of Mrs Blossom having taken their toll. Her head lolled against Katherine's shoulder, and now and then she snored. When she did, Katherine poked her sharply in the ribs which made her snort in surprise but settled her back into silence.

Katherine thought about what she had seen in Cherry Blossom's home. She wondered at what age Cherry first began to suspect that having flying ducks or birds on your walls was *not all right*. Once the suspicion became a certainty, how was she supposed to view the doting father and mother who put them there? Would she not begin to hold every aspect of her home life up to scrutiny? Surely she would quickly learn to deride the sentimental feeling that had caused her parents to plant the three cherry trees (and had not Mrs Blossom mentioned that there were many other threesomes in the house?). But just suppose, to compound the complexity of her feeling, she also realised, after the initial rejection of the décor in her parents' home, that the birds and other threesomes were in their own way rather pretty? Perhaps it would even be possible to think of the flying birds as beautiful?

Uneasy at her own thoughts, Katherine poked Moira who protested with a snort.

What would such conflicting feelings do to a bright adolescent girl, she wondered? First, she would stop wearing the pretty frocks loved by her parents, then she would cut her hair. Next she would try a direct onslaught by bringing her friends to stay and having them lounge around getting drunk and possibly smoking dope. Finally, she would cultivate the cult of the ugly, leave her Hansel and Gretel gingerbread home and change her name to Hilary Greep. What else could she do? Become a witch? Well, she had. She had cast her evil spell over her parents, leaving them frozen for ever in the house they had created as a setting for their princess, mourning her absence. The bad witch had gone away, and with a wave of her wand had created darkness where there had once been light, ugliness where there had once been beauty, and perversity where there had once been simplicity. Cherry Blossom's progress through life was a superb example of the making of an intellectual delinquent.

Chapter Ten

'Wouldn't it be convenient if she suffered from peanut allergy, or something like it. Then we could get rid of her quite innocently with a slice of cake,' Georgina said.

'Yes, wouldn't it,' Katherine said thoughtfully. They were having lunch in Belgrave Square; ham sandwiches and a half-bottle of champagne. Georgio was out on what he described as a business appointment. 'I suppose we could send Grace round to have tea with her again and ask. Goodness, this is a nice lunch,' she added. 'I hate restaurants, don't you?'

'Yes. There's all that awkwardness of moving around the tables and settling oneself. Then one probably wants to go to the loo which is always down a steep flight of stairs, and then one has to get back up again, which is probably quite all right for you, but not at all easy for me. By the time one has settled again at the table with one's napkin on one's knees and one of those silly, outsized menus in front of one, one probably wants to go again. It's much more comfortable to stay at home. Did you know Archie peed on one of my armchairs?'

'Yes, you told me.'

'There you are. It's much better to stay at home. It muddles the mind to move about too much. Georgio says I'm going gaga. Do you think it's possible?'

'I don't know. I do a memory exercise once a week. I'm told that it can slow down deterioration.'

'Oh dear, I expect I should be doing one too. It's just the sort of thing Grace should do.'

'I think her time would be better spent cultivating Miss Blossom.'

'I don't really see the point. There is nothing we can do to stop her writing her book. It will probably be as dry as dust, full of feminist jargon and contorted language. It will be perfectly turgid and die the death. If a few mad lesbians read it, it will hardly matter.'

'You can't be sure it will be unreadable; it's worth a peanut cake or some dubious oysters, I would think,' Katherine said lightly, twiddling her knife. She added, 'I would just like to get a look at some sample pages to make sure it's unreadable. Grace says that Chatto has shown some interest in it.'

'Perhaps we should trip her up on one of the spiral stair-cases leading down from the stacks in the London Library and break her neck,' Georgina suggested cheerfully.

'No guarantee of death,' Katherine pointed out. 'Breaking a few of her limbs would serve no useful purpose. Don't you remember Roger Poulton's car crash? Unconscious for a month and still he survived.'

'He wouldn't have been able to write a book after it.'

'That's true.' Katherine looked thoughtful.

'Katherine, stop it. You're making me uneasy. We can't harm that little girl.'

'Not so little, she's at least five foot six. Her parents had her measurements since the age of three on the

124

kitchen door. Useful for the coffin maker, one would think.'

'Stop it!'

'Stalin had Trotsky killed for less.'

Portia put back the telephone receiver. She stood in the hall muffled and cold. She did not know what to do with herself, where to go in her distress to be alone. Oh to be with Annabel in the Himalayas as she died. Annabel! Oh Annabel!

Portia went to her bedroom and locked the door connecting her room to Archie's, their marital bedroom. That room was large and light, with two long sash windows, a carpet and a pretty armchair in faded rose chintz. Her own room, once the dressing-room, now seemed claustrophobic, with its narrow bed, chest-of-drawers, scrap of rug on bare boards, and the two dull prints of a horse and a tiger on the wall. It was too monastic a setting in which to think about Annabel. To go back decade upon decade of memories, to re-invent the jokes and fights, to remember the naughtiness, the unforgettable naughtiness of youth, before marriages, lovers, and those coarsening small betrayals of the spirit took their toll on friendship. She closed her eyes, squeezing them tight, making herself feel dizzy. Then she sat upright and still on the edge of her iron bedstead. She pictured Annabel in a short-sleeved Aertex shirt and shorts, glowing with good health, shrugging off her husband after Bad Annabel went off with him all those years ago, children and flower borders, for the pleasure of donkeys, camels, deserts and mountains. A life lived so entirely in the present that the emotions of other people slid off her as water off a seal's skin. Including, in the history of their friendship, hers. She would not forget that in her sorrow. It was part of that sorrow.

125

She got to her feet, struggled into an extra jersey, her fingers whitened and clumsy with shock. Going down the back stairs to avoid Archie, she could hear him calling her, not by name (he never called her anything now) but just, 'Where are you? Where are you?' Quickly, she slipped out of the side door on the east side, and walked slowly across the fields to the wooded cliff, her limbs feeling as though they were part of the soggy ground. The weather was balmy. She would have had it roaring and wet, obliterating the all too familiar curves of the rocky coves below. She wanted a wild unfamiliar landscape, the right language in which to think about Annabel. She was suffocating in the domesticity Annabel had so conspicuously avoided when Bad Annabel ran off with her husband. Annabel had been lucky to die as she would have wished. It was unfair. She, Portia, was stuck, earth-bound, in the Somerset soil. Her family gave her little actual pleasure any more. And then there was Archie.

For an hour she sat, her stiffened legs outstretched on a grassy tuft, feeling Annabel's death in her own limbs. As her discomfort increased, thoughts of Archie intruded. He might well have wandered away by now. Should she ring the village and start scouring the woods, or do nothing and let him be? What, after all, was the point? If the villagers talked, there was little that could be added to what they already knew. And he had never failed to turn up yet. Even London could not lose him. The violent anxiety she felt when he was lost was the only emotional touchstone she had left to quicken the barren coolness of her feeling towards him. Mother birds would stuff an open purse for want of fledglings to feed when the season was upon them. Women were genetically programmed to look after the young and the very old. That was all her anxiety meant.

When she entered the kitchen she found Archie and Mrs Willis at the table. Mrs Willis was cutting up bread soldiers, and Archie was dunking them in a boiled egg.

'I know it's not really time for a meal,' Mrs Willis said, 'but it keeps him happy and contented. Doesn't it, Mr Sheldon? I just popped in to say hello and found him wandering around, up in the attics, calling.'

'What were you doing in the attics?' Portia asked sharply.

'I heard him calling from the hall, didn't I, Mr Sheldon? And wasn't he pleased to see me!'

'Mrs Willis found me,' Archie said, smiling with such happiness that Portia wanted to brain him.

'Archie, Annabel's dead. You remember Annabel, don't you?' Portia said to him, fetching a cup and saucer for herself.

'Mrs Willis found me,' Archie repeated.

'You remember Annabel. You particularly liked Annabel,' Portia said with emphasis.

'Yes, Annabel,' Archie said.

'She's dead.'

Archie said, 'Mrs Willis found me.'

'I am sorry,' Mrs Willis said. 'Has a friend died?'

Katherine heard the telephone ringing from the bathroom. Why, she wondered, does it always ring when one is on the lavatory? She had always rather enjoyed sitting on the lavatory ever since she was a child. Then she had locked herself into the bathroom for an hour at a time to read. It was the only place safe from interruption. She wouldn't hurry and spoil it, she decided. Of course it was spoilt. It had broken the reflective nature of the time spent there.

127

'Have you heard,' Georgina asked, when Katherine rang back. 'Annabel has died.'

'She can't have.' Katherine's voice was full of pain and shock. 'I only saw her yesterday and she was fine. I mean, she was as fine as she can be these days.'

'No, no. It's Good Annabel who has died. Who would have thought it? She was so stringy and supple. She always made me feel particularly decrepit. Who would have thought she would go before Bad Annabel?'

Katherine sat down, the painful tension suffusing her gradually draining from her limbs. Her clamped hand had difficulty relaxing its grip on the receiver. Her lips moved for a second as though forming words. 'I'm sorry. You shocked me. I thought Annabel had died.'

'I know, it is shocking, isn't it? Any of us could be snuffed out at any minute.'

'Georgina, is that all you can think about?'

'No. But it's impossible not to think about it, even as one thinks how sad it will be not to see her again. Ever since I heard the news I have been conscious of the job my heart is doing. I can hear it quite distinctly. It's making me feel quite unwell. I know if I am made to leave this house and move into a flat with a lift I shall die.'

'What are you talking about?'

'My son Christopher wants me to move out of the house and live in a flat. He owns the house, you know.'

'No. I didn't.'

'He's more difficult than his father was. How I didn't notice it when he was a boy, I can't imagine. I could have beaten it out of him then.'

'How did Annabel die?'

'A heart attack in the Himalayas.'

128

'Was she alone?'

'No. She was with Geoffrey and Molly Cardew. They've burnt her out there. In a great Hindu pyre. They will bring her ashes back when they finish their expedition. Apparently bringing her down proved too difficult. Can you imagine it!'

'I don't want to.'

'I wonder what happens about death certificates when you burn somebody in an impromptu manner on a hillside? Do you think we should tell Annabel that Good Annabel has died?'

'Yes. It cannot fail to interest her, and that is all that matters now. Anything to enliven bedside conversation. Presumably there will be a memorial service or something?'

'I expect so.'

'You can't trust her children. They considered she neglected them.'

'I thought you did not care if people attended your obsequies?'

'I don't care. But Annabel isn't me. Anyway, all these deaths are getting me down.'

'You mean Bad Annabel and Blanche?'

'And Cherry Blossom.'

'Stop it, Katherine.' Georgina made her voice cross and not – as she thought afterwards with satisfaction – frightened at all.

That evening as Georgina and Georgio sat in the upstairs sitting-room eating rarebit on their knees, Georgina turned the sound of the television down. 'Do you think, if one murdered someone, one would be haunted by it?'

'I think it might be more disagreeable than you might

think. Of course, how well you knew the person and the method you used would make a difference. Why? Who are you thinking of murdering?'

Gradually they had taken to having supper earlier and earlier. It was seven o'clock. At eight o'clock there was a thriller series on television to which Georgina was addicted. Georgio sometimes went out after supper.

'I'm not telling you. You might blackmail me.'

'It's not me, is it?'

'Have you done something I might murder you for?'

'I'm not sure,' Georgio said cautiously. 'Possibly. I've been meaning to bring it up.'

'Well?' Georgina's voice was light but she had a premonition of disaster. No wonder her heart had been sounding so odd all day. He's going to kill me, she thought. I mustn't let him say it. It'll kill me.

'Well?' she asked again.

'It's a question of money. I need some rather badly.'

'Have you noticed how people always cover violent feeling with "rather". You need some *rather* badly. What you mean is, hand some over, or else! Or else what?'

He looked down. 'Or else I'll tell you why I need it.' He put his half-eaten rarebit on the floor, kicked the plate a little way away from him, and lit a cigarette.

'And then I might murder you?'

'It's conceivable you might want to.'

'But you think I'll give you the money if I know the reason?'

'I don't know. I can only hope you might.'

'How much are we talking about?'

'Around ten thousand for the next couple of years.'

'That's a lot.'

Georgio did not say anything.

'My programme's beginning,' Georgina said. 'We'll talk about it afterwards. I can't afford that kind of money. I'm going to have to know the reason.'

'I think I should tell you now.'

'No. After the programme.' Georgina turned up the sound of the television.

Georgio went out.

Georgina was pleased to go to bed without seeing him again. She did not sleep well.

Five shrieking Pekinese were tied up to the railings outside the London Library. Seeing them, Moira knew she would find Katherine inside. She found her in the Reading Room surrounded by books. Sitting down beside her she swiftly scanned their titles: *Right-Wing Women* by Andrea Dworkin, *Gyn/Ecology* by Mary Daly, *Against Our Will* by Susan Brownmiller, and *Backlash: The Undeclared War Against Women* by Susan Faludi.

'She mentioned the authors. So I thought I would look at them on the adage of "know thy enemy",' Katherine whispered.

'I would have thought she had explained all that very clearly to us,' Moira whispered back.

'Most of the books consist of *News of the World*-style sex and horror stories. Porn without much rigour.' She changed the subject. 'I want you all to come back for lunch after Annabel's memorial service next Thursday. We need to discuss things if we are to turn Hilary Greep into harmless Cherry Blossom and it's too good an opportunity to miss as we will all be together.'

That evening Katherine wrote to Mrs Blossom. She had

thought about ringing her up, but she felt unable to discuss Cherry with her as though she cared about the girl when part of her mind was bent on her destruction.

Dear Mrs Blossom [she wrote],

I did enjoy meeting you when Moira and I were on our travels, and I have been thinking a lot about our conversation about Cherry. I do feel for you and I am sure that Cherry really loves you and your husband. I am sending you her address, and I think the best thing would be if you wrote to her every week showing her your love and your hurt, and reminding her of the good things in her childhood that had once given her pleasure. I think her life has become embittered, full of easy slogans to do with woman's place in the world, and she needs to be reminded about who she really is. I realise that your husband will have difficulty writing to her in this way as I expect he is very angry and hurt, so it is up to you. But for Cherry to be truly united to you it is VERY IMPORTANT THAT SHE IS RECONCILED WITH HER FATHER. I cannot tell you how vital this is. I write as the ex-headmistress of many girls. The relationship between daughters and their fathers is VITAL for their future well-being.

We will all work towards this end. Cherry's address is 303 Loftus Road, London W12.

With best wishes for a happy outcome.

Yours sincerely, Katherine Sackville

On finishing the letter, Katherine decided she had done her best to ensure the future physical well-being of Hilary Greep. If Hilary Greep could be persuaded to merge back into the innocent figure of Cherry Blossom with her long hair and party dress shown to her and Moira by Mrs Blossom, then the Pearls need not act. Hilary Greep's fate lay in Cherry Blossom's hands.

Annabel's memorial service took place at St Thomas's, Battersea, on June 12th. Mourners packed the red-brick Victorian church. Laura had considerable difficulty in manoeuvring Maisy's wheelchair to a place where there was no chance of someone accidentally sitting on her mother's lap.

Moira, arriving a few minutes late, had to ask a young man for his seat. Then she discovered there was no kneeler. It ruffled her spirits.

Laura had better luck. As she knelt during the prayers on the wooden floor in the right-hand aisle, a man, without a glance in her direction, passed his kneeler to her. She was as pleased with the gracefulness of the action as Moira was displeased with the manners of modern man.

Portia, coming up from Somerset on a cheap day ticket, sat beside Katherine in a far back pew. She found it difficult to concentrate on the service because Katherine had told her she expected her to stay for lunch afterwards.

'It is too good an opportunity, with every able-bodied member of the group present, not to thrash out what we are going to do about Hilary Greep,' she had said.

Portia wondered how she was going to manage. She had intended to catch the three-thirty back to Taunton. That would no longer be possible. Would she be able to catch the six-thirty? In that case she would not arrive until a quarter to nine and not reach home until half-past nine. If she failed to catch that train, then everything would be an hour later. She had left Archie in Anna's charge, but Anna was going to a poetry recital in Minehead and could hardly take Archie with her. If she didn't, she was bound to ask Mrs Willis to look after him. Anna did not understand that Mrs Willis was not a suitable person to have charge of Archie. When she explained that Mrs Willis took advantage of him, Anna said, 'How can she? He's happy with her and it's not as if he can sign anything away. The poor darling's never owned anything.'

> From Greenland's icy mountains,
> From India's coral strand,
> Where Afric's sunny fountains
> Roll down their golden sand . . .

At the start of the hymn only the old voices in the congregation sang with thin certainty. Katherine's still rich contralto lent a depth to her side of the church that would otherwise have been quavery. By the second stanza, the rest of the congregation took up the rollicking tune:

> What though the spicy breezes
> Blow soft o'er Java's isle,
> Though every prospect pleases
> And only man is vile:
> In vain with lavish kindness
> The gifts of God are strown;
> The heathen in his blindness
> Bows down to wood and stone.

By the third verse the congregation could have been accused of enthusiasm:

Can we, whose souls are lighted
With wisdom from on high,
Can we to men benighted
The lamp of life deny . . .

They all sat down, Katherine ramrod straight. She believed good deportment took years off her actual age. She thought Portia had aged since she last saw her. Perhaps the realisation that she would never walk with Annabel again in the mountainous pathways of Tibet or Kurdistan – although it must be twenty years since the two of them had done the latter – had finally tightened her joints. She needed to be jolted, to have her bones cracked, to have electrodes stimulate the nerve ends. Katherine touched Portia on the shoulder, whether in benediction or warning she was not sure. Portia looked at her. Katherine was looking very well, she thought. She was wearing her black, wide-brimmed, straw Mainboucher hat. Thirty years ago, when she had first worn it at Lavinia Seagrave's wedding to Peter Petherick, she had looked like an elegant black-and-white bean-pole. Today it looked just as fitting at Annabel's requiem.

Peter Sturrage, retired Bishop of Cirencester, stood in the modern manner facing the congregation to the right of the altar:

My dear brethren, we are gathered here to bear witness
to the life of Annabel Bennet and to mourn her death.
We all knew and loved her. It is difficult to think of
her as dead. Like myself, many of you here will have
accompanied her on one of her travels to far-flung and
exotic places. As the hymn we have just been singing
somewhat quaintly put it, 'From Greenland's icy

135

mountains/ From India's coral strand/ Where Afric's sunny fountains/ Roll down their golden sand.' Perhaps she was not quite the missionary the hymn suggests, but in her own way Annabel was like the missionaries of old. When in early middle age she found it necessary to change her life, she, like Joan of Arc before her, left her pots and pans to others and took her destiny into her own hands. Though, in her case, it was to venture out and meet the peoples of the world rather than embrace the bloody, nationalistic agenda of Joan of Arc. Although she may not have preached the word of God, her presence in those far-flung places gave of the very best that England has to offer – a woman of discernment who behaved with humour, courtesy and dignity. She did not abuse her hosts in these far-flung places by inappropriate dress or decorum. In fact, she was, in all she did, a Western ambassadress. She celebrated the differences between lands and cultures. In God's eyes, I think, her mission must have been blessed. Now she has embarked on a new adventure, with different signposts and a different language, but who could possibly doubt that her pilgrimage will be triumphantly successful? I, for one, hope that I will find her guiding hand on that rocky mountain pass when my time comes to take my staff in hand, and venture forth into territory I have only read about in the Bible. So let us now join together and sing with heartfelt joy 'To Be a Pilgrim'.

As the congregation launched themselves into the first lines suitably adapted to fit the occasion:

Who would true valour see,
Let her come hither;
One here will constant be,
Come wind, come weather . . .

Katherine said to Portia through the singing, 'All that guff was to get round the fact that Annabel did not have a religious bone in her body.'

'Oh, I don't know,' Portia demurred in a whisper. 'When she stayed with me she spent hours locked in her bedroom meditating and levitating. She often got lift-off.'

'Did you look through the keyhole? Did you see her rise off the ground?'

'You are worse than St Thomas.'

They joined in the singing.

'"Let us pray,"' the Bishop intoned. Katherine and Portia concentrated on the service . . .

A man with an exceedingly good head of white fluffy hair went to the chancel.

He had a soft, plump, papery complexion and very clear blue eyes. He was around eighty. 'The family have asked me to say that you are all welcome in the crypt for a light lunch.' Then, clicking his heels together and raising his arm, he added, 'Heil Hitler.'

The congregation was profoundly startled.

'It's the sort of thing that gives old age a bad name,' Moira said as they comforted themselves afterwards with champagne and potted shrimps on toast in Katherine's large yellow drawing-room. She was sitting bolstered by a cushion in a deep armchair.

Katherine's flat was so resplendently big that Grace wondered why they had never used it to meet in before.

'He's a very old friend of Annabel's. Godfather to one of the children,' Portia explained. 'He was one of Mosley's black-shirts before the war. Recently the enthusiasms of his youth seem to have overtaken him again. Annabel's family left him in charge of designing the memorial service because he wanted to do it so badly. And he absolutely promised that there would be no mention of politics. They weren't sure if he was to be trusted, but in the end you have to take risks, don't you?'

'It's about risk-taking that I want to talk to you all,' Katherine said as she led the way to the dining-room.

Moira wheeled Maisy in and set her at the head of the table. Her instinct told her that it might be best if Katherine did not command the table. She placed herself at the other end. Georgina wondered, as she sat herself down, whether she was the only one who had some idea of what Katherine intended to propose. Risk-taking indeed! Drink was the thing, she decided, and perhaps barracking noises.

'Portia, you must have felt at home,' Moira said, deflecting the conversation from risk-taking. 'The service was full of Annabel's aristocratic friends . . .'

And me, Maisy thought to herself. They always forget where I come from.

'And hats. Have you ever seen so many hats!'

'I'm not sure Portia's hat could be considered particularly distinguished,' said Katherine, thinking of her own.

'No. But Grace's can. Grace, your hat is lovely,' Moira said.

'I wore it because Annabel once admired it. It's very old.' Grace's hat was a soft, dark, glowing green velvet, and had a dark-red flower in the same material on one side.

The food, all from Harrods, looked glossy. Katherine had emptied the salads into bowls and laid out the meats and the salmon mousse on dishes. She felt pleased with herself. Percy was in the kitchen, slowly washing up the glasses and cutlery as they appeared. Over the years Katherine had worked out the exact rate at which things should move from the dining-room into the kitchen so that Percy should not be overwhelmed. An internal clock in her head ticked away no matter what was going on around her. It was one of the reasons she had been such an efficient chairman of meetings. On the whole she sent things out in twos and threes without her guests being aware of the production line they formed. Percy and Katherine had always worked well as a team.

'This is as good as Grace in her Mayfair days. Why have we never had meetings here before?' Moira asked.

'Yes, why?' Grace repeated.

'Grace had staff. I only have Percy.'

'When are we going to talk about Hilary Greep?' Maisy enquired.

Katherine thought Maisy was tucking into the food with unattractive relish.

Maisy was hungry. Laura was on a diet and her method of keeping to a diet was to serve such boring food that she was not tempted to eat much. The diet consisted of a piece of poached chicken and salad seven days a week. Maisy was given the same. Laura ate no lunch but allowed her mother a tin of red kidney beans, for the roughage. 'Nobody,' she said virtuously to her brother John, 'would be able to accuse me of not keeping Mother healthy!'

Maisy had come to hate red kidney beans.

'We'll talk about Miss Blossom with our coffee,' Katherine replied with firmness.

'Let's talk about Annabel,' Maisy suggested. 'It is why we are all here.'

'At least she was supple to the end. What more can you want than that – and, of course, having all your marbles,' Georgina said.

Chocolate mousse could only be eked out so long. Percy shouted that the coffee was in the drawing-room and the Pearls reluctantly filed back, ready now to discuss what they should do about Hilary Greep, and her destruction of Charlotte M. Yonge's reputation.

Grace handed out the coffee as Katherine poured.

'Pearls, I think we all agree that Hilary Greep has to be stopped from producing her biography.' Katherine looked around at them benignly.

'I don't see what we can do to stop her,' Portia said.

'Katherine thinks she should have a little accident,' Georgina said drily.

There was an uneasy silence.

'Oh no!' Grace exclaimed.

'It's war,' Katherine said.

'What do you mean, war?'

Katherine made a movement, encompassing them. 'Between people like us – our generation – and them, the Goths!'

There was another silence.

'Our generation has hung a good deal on to the idea of duty. Charlotte M. Yonge led a very dutiful life. Her novels ask what man owes to God's law, and the answer, for her, is everything. I don't believe in God. I would be surprised if deep down many of you do either. What I do believe in is Truth. I believe in the laws of Truth. For better or worse, our lives are what we have made of them in the sight of man. What value has our existence if *that* truth can be played about with by others for their own ends. In any examination of our lives there are things that one would hope a sympathetic examiner would not linger upon unduly. Take Blanche, for instance. If Maisy were to write her biography, a picture would emerge which would be instantly recognisable to us all: a tall, big-boned woman with her hair in a bun, a scientist of small discoveries and much microscopic work, a convinced Christian who put science at the centre of God's universe, a woman of sense and rigour, a loving mother in partnership with a dull husband . . .'

'Slow down, Katherine; I'm not at all sure that is how I see her,' Maisy said.

'But suppose,' Katherine continued, 'at the same time a doctor decided to use her life as a case study of a stroke victim. A completely unrecognisable picture might well appear. It would all be headaches, high blood pressure, internal organs, chuntering liquids, twinges of indigestion and the stress of her career. He might pay particular attention to her diet – discover a secret addiction to chocolate, a craving for salt. Then he would discuss her as she is today with her incontinence, bed sores, and snoring. I know that I, for one, would be extremely indignant at her being used in such a way – but not quite so indignant as I would be had the subject been Georgina or myself. There is always the possibility that Blanche, being a scientist, might not object to her life being interpreted mechanically. But even if she didn't, it would still be a travesty of the life she really lived. It would be a life that robbed her of her actions, thoughts and feelings, one that her children and grandchildren would not recognise – nor, for that matter, would her laboratory assistant. Everybody dies badly. Death is at best grotesque, usually it is humiliating and painful. Would any of us wish for the summation of our lives to be in our deaths? Or even in the gradual humiliating decline of our old age . . .?'

141

Portia thought of Archie.

'All we have left to us at the end of the day is our reputation, or, if not that, the truth of our life as we lived it. Our truth will of course differ from the perceptions of others who have known us. For instance, Georgina's experience of motherhood might well differ from her children's perception of her as a mother. A just biographer would accept and understand both points of view. Yet another biographer might well have a much harsher view of Georgina as a mother. But however they present her, they should be working from the known facts about Georgina in that role.

'Hilary Greep has developed out of a completely different culture. She could come from Mars. Although only around fifty years divide us from her, the cultural gulf is greater than that which divides us from the Ancient Greeks. I have gleaned from my devoted reading of the art critic of the *Daily Telegraph* that this new phenomenon and the people who belong to it are described as "post-human". As you can see, I have been doing a lot of reading since meeting Miss Greep. In this brave new world there is no dividing line between reality and non-reality. Each has equal weight. A real vice-president of the United States will appear in a television soap opera talking about the fictional concerns of fictional characters as though he were addressing real issues in front of real people, and he will win or lose votes by the way he conducts himself on television. To a proportion of the viewers, he and the fiction he is entering into have the same reality. Like bubonic plague.' She came to a stop.

'What about bubonic plague?' Moira asked, bewildered.

'I don't know. It just came into my head.'

She really is going a bit funny, Georgina thought.

'I don't think you can harm someone because their thought

142

processes are alien. It would be a bit like being a racist.' Moira spoke aggressively.

'We killed Nazis because their thought processes were obnoxious. This is war.'

'This is not war. Governments can declare war. Individuals merely murder people.'

'This is guerrilla warfare.'

'I was a magistrate for twenty years,' Portia protested.

'I know, darling,' Katherine explained. 'But that was a duty to your ancestral past. This is real life.'

'This is ridiculous. I wish Blanche were here. She'd put a stop to this silly conversation in a trice.' Portia's soft voice took on a tone unfamiliar to any but Katherine. 'I am a committed Christian and a member of the Church of England. You do not harm someone because they hold opinions and do things you don't like. If possible, you send them to prison or sue them, but that's it. In Hilary Greep's case we can't do either and that is that.'

'Portia, I know you go to church and I'm sure you pray. But when you go knock, knock, who's there? don't you think that what you get is a reflection of your own wishes?'

'We are too old to play those games,' Portia said. 'They're for undergraduates. I'm going to die sometime in the next fifteen years and I don't want to go to hell.' She turned to the others. 'I have never quite realised it before, but I think Katherine is wicked. She probably always has been wicked but it's never cropped up before.'

'You mean I have never wanted to murder anybody before?' Katherine suggested.

'Murder isn't the only wicked thing people do. You might well have demonstrated your wickedness all over the place but living in the country I never noticed.'

'Or maybe it has been lying dormant in you. Grace and I were discussing it the other day,' Georgina said.

'You're probably right.'

'No. No. Of course, Katherine hasn't always been wicked. This is just a little aberration because she isn't sitting on any committees any more,' Moira said soothingly.

'I just want you all to go away and think about it. We don't need to make a decision immediately but we do have to decide on something before Moira returns to her island haven. Think about yourselves and those of whom you are fond. Think how near death you are. Any of us could pop off like Annabel at any moment. Think hard about whether you really believe in an afterlife – or if you believe like me that the good and evil you do on this earth are all that remains after death. The Hilary Greeps of the world have declared war on man's vested interest in truth and how we are to be judged by our peers hereafter. I propose we strike a blow for that essential morality. All I ask is that you go away and think about it.'

Relieved, they said they would do just that, and with the exception of Maisy, who had to wait for Laura to collect her, they made hurried farewells. Maisy, exhausted by unfamiliar thinking, fell into a light sleep, while Katherine and Percy cleared away the debris of Annabel's memorial feast.

Chapter Eleven

Maisy was not the only Pearl who nodded off after lunch at Katherine's flat. Georgina did too. She felt so odd when she arrived back at Belgrave Square that she tipped the taxi driver too much. She found she could not work out twelve and a half per cent of seven pounds forty-six pence. Her mind gabbled at her. She found herself thinking about half-a-crowns. How you always tipped half-a-crown. Half-a-crown was two-and-six but what was two-and-six? For the life of her, she couldn't remember. She rounded the figure up and gave the driver nine pounds. She knew it was too much. Once in the house, she called for Georgio, and felt unexpectedly lonely when she realised he was not there. It proved you shouldn't leave the house. She didn't usually feel lonely when alone. It was coming back to an empty house that made you feel lonely.

It took her longer than usual to climb the stairs. It was not just that the pain of her suppurating legs made her pause on each step, but that her limbs felt heavy with exhaustion. She made more of an effort when Georgio was there, even if he was doing whatever he did in his office at the top of the house. Once in the sitting-room she turned on the television and sank into her chair. Not for a moment did she think of what had taken place at Katherine's lunch. Within seven minutes she was asleep.

Grace had a sleepless night. Maybe she was going mad. Sometimes she thought she was asleep because when she closed her eyes, there was Katherine, a monster teacher brandishing a cane. Georgina and she were little girls in her class. Their task was to pick nettle leaves and turn them into gold. Sometimes they were at their desks (this was when the cane came swishing through the air towards the palms of their hands), at other times they were in a field leaning over a ditch filled with nettles. Either way they were going to be hurt. I am seventy-seven years old, Grace told herself. I cannot be made to do anything. But I can, I can, she cried to herself as her vision see-sawed between the green field and the brown desk. I am always being made to do things I don't want to do. Georgina, she pleaded, don't let it happen. If only Blanche were around. Grace knew she was not dreaming because when she got up in the morning she felt so terrible. Coffee at seven o'clock improved things a little. Night-time was always the worst. The worst things seemed possible then. Of course nobody was really going to hurt that pretty girl who had given her tea.

Before going out at ten o'clock to visit Robert she rang Fortnum & Mason and ordered a large cellophaned concoction of preserved fruits to be sent to Hilary Greep with a message saying 'Thank you for being so sweet and giving me tea. With best wishes for your continued good health, Grace.' She did not put her surname, just in case. She realised that Hilary Greep might be a little surprised at receiving her gift as it was now more than a month since she had visited her, but old ladies were allowed to do things slowly. It was one of their prerogatives.

She was still feeling a little shaky when she entered Robert's room. Ready tears filled her eyes at the dear, familiar sight of him lying there breathing strenuously. She slipped her hand under the sheet and finding the slit in his pyjamas happily grasped the warm reassuring flesh that quivered within her palm. She told him about Annabel's funeral and the lunch at Katherine's flat and, lowering her voice, of Katherine's outrageous suggestion that they should murder Hilary Greep. Suddenly, the semi-flaccid flesh engorged, and a pole, knotted like some great oak, rose. Shocked, she withdrew her hand and looked at the face, at the eyes half hidden by the lids and the rigid open mouth that was now merely a breathing machine. The breath was coming more quickly now. 'How could you? How could you?' she said, as though to a naughty child. 'You are as bad as Katherine. Really, Robert. This isn't some fantasy, it's real. Katherine really intends that we should do it.'

Upset by Robert's reaction to the news, she cut short her visit and, hoping to be soothed, went shopping. She liked to visit Fortnum & Mason every three weeks or so. Once you left the food hall on the ground floor it was not crowded, and the saleswomen were happy to chat as you tried on shoes and examined handbags and scarves. She bought a pair of fawn-coloured shoes with little sturdy heels. Recently, she had begun to feel a little insecure when coming down the rather narrow staircase at home. She had even stopped taking her evening sherry up to her bath.

She had a nice chat with the woman who served her. The shop assistant lived in Clapham and her daughter was training to be a hairdresser. There was the possibility that one day she

147

might work in the hairdressing salon at Fortnum & Mason. That would be nice, Grace thought, and decided to have a sandwich in the less crowded café upstairs before going home. Once settled with a chicken sandwich and a glass of white wine, thoughts of Robert came flooding back. It was obvious that he understood everything going on around him. She thought with shame of the way she had fallen into telling him the most trivial complaints, and had talked out her thoughts as though she were the only witness to them. It was not as though she had not been given a sign that he was not in a vegetable state. She had even told him of the anxiety she felt about her thinning hair and how she hated seeing her brush after passing through it, and how her hairdresser could not summon up even polite condolences when she tried to discuss the state of her hair with him. Putting rollers in old women's hair obviously bored him. But she paid him to tease it, pat it, tell her it looked fine, and recommend tonics and thickening shampoos. As she thought about the injustice of her hairdresser's behaviour, tears pricked her eyes. She should move on. Perhaps she should try the salon at Fortnum's? What, oh what should she do about Robert? She could not tell the nurses of her discovery. Dismay and excitement meshed together and gradually blotted out thoughts of her hair, the revitalising skin tonic she was contemplating trying, and what she should buy for supper before leaving Fortnum's. She thought of Robert lying there, bored out of his mind, and then of telling him of Katherine's wish to murder Hilary Greep and the surge of excitement that possessed his body. What should she do? Oh dear, Katherine was a very wicked woman!

Moira also slept when she returned from lunch at Katherine's flat. She took off her dress and climbed into bed. Awakening at drinks time, she decided she could not face going out to dinner that evening. She was to have been one of three guests of a bachelor friend in his sixties whose friends were older women and younger men. She rang him and cried off. It was a privilege of age. She had, she felt, had enough entertainment for one day. That night she slept badly. She longed to be in Saint-Barthélemy with her cat. The following day she rang Georgina and proposed that they should meet with Maisy to discuss things privately. Georgina suggested they come round to her, but when told of the plan Laura said it would be a lot easier if Georgina and Moira came to them. She would cook. Georgina was not pleased. She thought her life was becoming unattractively restless. She hoped nobody else would die soon, including Hilary Greep.

When she told Georgio she was going out the following Tuesday he announced that he would also be out that night. Ever since he had told her he wanted money for a reason that might make her want to murder him, Georgina had eyed Georgio's comings and goings with suspicion.

'Where are you going?' she asked.

They were downstairs in the large drawing-room having a bowl of tinned onion soup for lunch. Georgio had made some delicious sandwiches of marinated peppers and aubergine.

'I am afraid we should discuss whether you are going to give me the money I mentioned to you the other day.'

'Are the two things connected? Where you are going for dinner and the money?'

'In a way.' Georgio's eyes slid around the room as though absent-mindedly. Patting his pockets, he took out his cigarettes.

'You are going to have to tell me why you want it.' Don't

149

give me a heart attack; please don't let it be anything *very* bad, Georgina pleaded to herself.

'I have a son. He has got himself into a bit of a pickle, been in court on breaking and entering charges. It's drugs, of course. I thought that perhaps he should go to Broadlands as it seems to have done such a good job on Robina and then I want him to go out to Australia and go to architectural school. Temptation is much less if you drop your previous friends. It's all going to cost a bit.'

'What do you mean you've got a son! How old is he?'

'Twenty.'

'You mean he was born since we were together.'

'Yes.'

'At the very beginning of our relationship?'

'Yes, but it's not quite what you think,' Georgio said defensively.

'What *do* I think?'

'You think while I was saying how much I loved you, I was having an affair with another woman.'

'And you weren't?' Georgina asked sarcastically.

'No.' Georgio was unable to go on.

'But you have a twenty-year-old son?'

'Yes.'

'Miraculous conception. With you acting as God the Father?'

'No.' Georgio re-lit his cigarette. 'I never got round to telling you when I met you, as it didn't seem relevant, that I was married.'

Georgina had nothing to say. Her mind told her nothing. In her surprise she felt nothing.

'She's called Maria.' He wondered if he should have said her name. It might have been better to leave her as a nameless fact.

150

'Are you divorced?'

'No. It didn't seem necessary – important. You know.'

'No, I don't.'

'It wasn't as though you and I were getting married or anything. It seemed a bit unfair to upset her. Maria's a Catholic. She wouldn't have liked to be divorced.'

'Is she in Greece?'

'No. Stockwell.'

'You're still seeing her.' It was a statement. Georgina was beginning to understand.

'The children were young. It would have been difficult for her on her own. She found it quite difficult in any case. She didn't know any English.'

'Children!' Georgina's voice rose to a screech.

It was Georgio's turn to be silent.

'How many children do you have?'

'Three.'

'You have three children. And you are married. And they all live in Stockwell.'

'No. Only Maria lives in Stockwell. They are all grown up. My daughter is married. She lives in Manchester. They were only little, five and six, when we came to England. Aeneas was the only one born over here.'

'You brought them over at the same time as you moved in with me?'

Georgio's left leg started to vibrate. He put his hands on it to try and gentle it down. 'Some months later. It was very expensive. They lived in Victoria then.'

'So I paid for them to come over?'

'Not entirely. A man owed me some money he could not pay, and in lieu of payment he gave me a key to a council flat.

151

That was what made it possible. They've been re-housed a few times since then.'

'And I've been keeping them ever since.'

'Not entirely. Maria used to get single mother allowance. Nowadays she works at a Greek restaurant. Of course, I help out a bit.'

'You mean I help out.'

'Georgina, I couldn't just leave her. It would have been heartless. And I love the children.'

'Why couldn't you have told me?'

'At the beginning I thought you would think I was coming with too much baggage and be put off. Afterwards it seemed unnecessary to have the row. They were settled and we were comfortable. If this problem hadn't arisen there was no reason why it shouldn't have continued to work perfectly well.'

'Until I died.' She repeated through clenched teeth, 'Until I died!' The humiliation of it melted her insides. 'How old is she?' she asked. 'After I die, what were you going to do? Move into her council flat? You wouldn't have had this place. You couldn't have moved your brood in here. Whatever happens when I die Christopher will throw you out. Were you relying on my having left you an annuity? I never left you anything outright, you know. I never trusted you. An annuity would have died with you, you know.' She was beside herself with rage. She no longer knew what she was saying. She wanted to throw herself about. She forgot about her creaky, painful joints. She felt herself rise to strike him. Only she didn't rise. Another self was afloat. She remained marooned in her chair. Abuse flowed out of her like lava. Words she never used before, words she hardly knew she knew.

Georgio left the house.

*   *   *

152

The following day Katherine rang and said she wished to have lunch with her.

'You'll have to bring it,' Georgina said. 'There's nothing in the house. Georgio has gone off somewhere. I'm not expecting him. It's not Percy's day.'

'I'll bring some sandwiches. It's really a working lunch. What do you like inside them?'

'Avocado and bacon.'

'I'm not sure I can achieve that. What's your second favourite?'

'Banana.'

'Mashed, or sliced?'

'Mashed.'

Unable to contemplate Georgina eating two mashed banana sandwiches without a shudder, Katherine also bought her a ham sandwich. She had tongue with mustard.

They munched them with a glass of wine in the upstairs sitting-room.

'My teeth can only cope with the likes of Mother's Pride, nowadays. How about yours?' Georgina asked.

'I've excellent bridge work.'

'It's not the bridge work that's the trouble, it's the gums.'

'I'm not discussing gums or any other aspect of human decay. It is how you present yourself that counts.'

'Very American.'

Sitting there, the two of them seemed so sensible, pleasant and ordinary that Georgina thought of telling Katherine about Georgio's family. But she did not. She felt she might lose the solid foundation of her being if she exposed herself to Katherine's uneasy concern.

'As you might expect,' Katherine said, 'I've been turning

over a few ideas in my mind about what we should do about Hilary Greep. And I thought it might be sensible to go over them together before putting them to the others. Two heads being better than one, and all that.'

'Why my head? Why not Moira's?'

'Moira drinks. It makes her unreliable.' Katherine thought that Moira might be the most difficult to persuade.

'Moira rang me. She wants to meet with Maisy and me to discuss your sanity. We can't allow you to hurt that girl.'

'Whatever is to be done will, of course, only be done with the consent of all the Pearls. I am merely formulating some ideas for us to consider.' She leaned forward, clasping Georgina's hands, nearly upsetting the plate from her lap, and said, 'Haven't you ever wished to do something seriously reckless which might actually affect something somewhere?'

'I suppose so,' Georgina said doubtfully, unaware that many people would consider that she had lived her life sublimely unaware of the consequences of her actions.

'Most people behave themselves because they are fearful of the law, or else because they are conditioned to do so by society, or by thoughts of divine retribution. Nowadays, of course, society hardly exists, which gives the Hilary Greeps of the world a free hand. Sometimes young people, who are inclined to think they are immortal until they are thirty, do unexpected things – like Joan of Arc – but mostly they just travel. Nobody thinks of the old as reckless, but they should. Like the young, but for opposite reasons, they have nothing to lose. The old have lost whatever power they might once have possessed through position, beauty or the command of children. They are lumped together, legislated over, and are at the mercy and the condescension of others. Younger people think they know better for no other reason than they

154

have firm flesh. It is quite disgusting when you think about it!' She spoke with such warmth and had such light in her eyes that Georgina felt her own cloudy eyes fill with tears.

Georgina disengaged her hands and blew her nose. 'Christopher is trying to get me out of here and move me into a mansion block with a lift. Georgio . . .' She stopped. Her mouth clamped shut, and her sinews became rigid beneath their covering of paper-thin skin.

'There, you see!'

'I can't kill Hilary Greep because Christopher is trying to evict me from my home.'

'I don't see why not, although I can think of a better reason for killing Hilary Greep. Come on, Georgina. It's now or never to strike a blow for truth, decency, moral rectitude and Charlotte M. Yonge.'

'Katherine!'

'Forget about decency then. I agree that decency is probably a red herring, but I do seriously think that, especially as one would be sacrificing so little, truth and moral rigour are probably worth the possibility of slopping out in Holloway Prison. Also I am planning for us to get away with it.'

'With what?'

'With whatever we decide to do with Hilary Greep.'

All the way down in the train to Taunton after the lunch with Katherine, Portia felt ruffled and angry. How dare Katherine hijack Annabel's funeral to propose an asinine scheme to kill Hilary Greep? How would she like it if they used the occasion of her funeral to discuss a wildlife sanctuary in the East End or something, instead of meeting together conscious of their friendship with her. She was outrageous, wicked. It wasn't as though Annabel had been a very dedicated Pearl who might

155

have entered into the occasion in spirit. She attended a meeting less than once a year and had never addressed them. Although she claimed to re-read *Dynevor Terrace* every few years.

All thoughts of Annabel vanished when she drove up to Sheldon Hall tired and hungry. There were two police cars outside the house. Archie, she thought, Archie, as she hurried, tripping up the steps to enter the hall. Voices came from the kitchen. Archie was sitting in one of the two wooden kitchen chairs with arm-rests, while Anna was standing behind him with her arms flung protectively around him, one of her hands fiddling with his hair. There were four policemen.

'He was just trying to find the loo, wee-wees, weren't you, darling,' Anna was saying.

Archie's face was alive with interest. He looked perfectly intelligent.

'Mummy!' Anna said gladly. 'Thank God you're here. They want to take poor Daddy away and lock him up!'

'What's happened?' Portia asked.

'Too silly . . .' Anna began but was interrupted.

'There has been a complaint,' one of the policemen told her. 'Apparently he exposed himself to two little girls. They were very upset and so are their parents.'

'They hit him. Poor Daddy. It's they who should be arrested!' Anna gently turned her father's head so that Portia could see the other side of it. His lip and cheek were swollen. Portia was frightened by the intelligence in his eyes. It was as though a fog had cleared in front of him. It was the wrong time.

She took off her coat, explaining as she did so, 'My husband is not well. He suffers from Alzheimer's disease. It affects his memory and other things. He cannot be held responsible for his actions. Where did it happen?'

'I am afraid it couldn't be worse, madam. He walked into a house in the village at eight-fifteen this evening. Mr Morris, the householder, had left the front door open because he was carrying articles to and fro from the garage. Mr Sheldon went upstairs to the kiddies' bedroom, opened the door, sat on their bed, pulled it out and asked them if they would like to touch it.'

It would be the Morrises, she thought. They were an aggressively self-righteous pair, difficult tenants who thought her condescending because she did not invite them to the Hall for a drink. 'Oh dear, it must have been very upsetting,' she said in a soft tut-tutting voice. 'Where do we go from here?' she asked, trying to include the police in what she wished them to see as a medical problem.

One of the other policemen spoke. 'We will have to charge him. The court will decide what to do.'

'It's a farce. He won't be able to plead,' Anna said furiously.

'I think Mr Sheldon should accompany us to the police station. We will call in our doctor to look at him and decide where to go from there.'

'Look, why don't I ring our doctor,' Portia suggested, 'and ask him to meet us in Watchet? He knows Archie and how ill he is.'

The police looked at each other and then the nice one said, 'Why not. We can't promise anything, though. The charge is serious. The family is very upset.'

'Of course we understand that, and of course we realise how upsetting it must have been for the Morrises' children, although are you quite sure it happened exactly as you described it? Archie does have a bad habit of pulling it out

157

of his trousers, but he has never asked anyone to touch it before.'

'You mean he has a history of exposing himself?'

'Only since his illness.'

One of the policemen wrote in his notebook. Neither Portia nor Anna liked that. Should she have denied the charge outright, Portia wondered, as Anna was obviously doing when she arrived? It would have been stupid. A few enquiries in the village would have revealed all.

After ringing their doctor and arranging for him to meet them at the police station, Portia asked if she could drive Archie in. 'He must be finding everything very muddling at the moment.'

'He doesn't look in the least muddled,' the policeman who had written in his notebook said.

Archie smiled at him. He had a particularly sweet smile.

'He seems to understand perfectly well what's happening.'

'It's the shock. He's not used to being hit,' Portia said.

'He didn't ought to have done what he did,' the policeman said.

Archie smiled at him again and looked delighted. He turned to Portia. 'A bad man hit me, look,' he said.

'I know, darling. You shouldn't have been doing what you were doing. We have to go to the police station.' She put out her hand to stroke him on the head as Anna had done. He flinched away from her touch. 'Can I drive him?' she asked again.

'No. He must come with us,' the nice policeman said. 'You can follow in your car if you wish.'

Following the police car, with Anna driving, they quarrelled violently. Portia was very hungry and as always under those circumstances filled with irritable anger.

'How could you let this happen! How could you let him wander down to the village like that! Do you realise what this means? They're going to charge him. They are going to make him stand up in court and they are going to recite all that filth. That revolting, self-important Mr Morris will tell that lie about him asking the girls to touch it. Archie would never have said that. He just thinks it's nicer out than in. Poor Archie. You have shamed your father. And me.'

'I was doing my dance exercises. He was watching quite happily. I didn't see him go. That's all. It's not as though he hasn't taken it out in the village before. He does it all the time. _You_ never stop him.'

'He should have been having his supper. I expect he was hungry and that was why he wandered off down there. They were probably cooking something in that house and it smelled good. That was why he went in. Why didn't you make him his supper? You are entirely selfish and self-absorbed.'

'I wasn't supposed to be making him his supper. You were supposed to be back. As it was, I had to cancel going into Minehead for the poetry reading. I was expecting you three hours ago. Why didn't you ring? That's what I call being selfish.' Anna amazed herself. She never answered her mother back. It was a rule that you didn't upset Mummy. They all loved her and according to their lights obeyed her vaguely uttered but steely rules.

Archie was held separately from them. They sat on a bench in the reception area not knowing what to do. When Maurice Catchpole, their doctor, arrived, Portia was close to tears.

'Don't worry too much,' he said. 'We'll sort it out.'

To the police he said, 'It's a difficult one. The Morrises

159

are also patients of mine. They have already been on to me talking about trauma. I expect they'll ring the press.'

The policeman looked vague. He had already rung the *Somerset Free Press* himself. There should, he reckoned, be a tenner in it.

Personally, Dr Catchpole thought exposure very overrated. There was something wrong with someone left in emotional disarray by the sight of a piece of flesh possessed by half the population, little boys and bare babies. It was the intention of the act that was threatening, and he doubted that Archie Sheldon had asked the girls to touch it. As far as he could gather, Archie did not get excited. After some discussion the police agreed to report Mr Sheldon for a summons. They felt the charge was too serious merely to caution him.

Dr Catchpole explained to Portia and Anna, 'It's not too bad. He is to be reported for a summons, but all being well they will not actually issue it. It will depend on the assessment of a social worker and a psychiatrist. I will explain the course his illness has taken. Meanwhile he can return to the Hall, but I am afraid questions may be asked about the long-term suitability of his staying at home if they think you are unable to control him. But we will tackle that when it arises. Nobody nowadays wants to spend money committing people to care unless there is no alternative. Be tactful with the social worker. Some of them are perfectly capable, but others need careful handling.'

The following day a reporter called. He had already called on the Morrises in the village. They had not allowed him to interview the children but had given him a photograph taken a year previously of them holding hands in their party frocks. They looked very sweet.

160

Portia had another row with Anna. She ordered her not to talk to any reporters.

'But, darling,' Anna tried to explain, 'I know quite a lot of them. I can probably plead with them not to run it, or play it down.'

'You will not succeed in doing anything of the sort. They will use you. Probably run a photograph of you doing something silly if they fail to get Archie. Your father's whole life is going to be summed up in this one incident. There is no fairness left, just cruelty and sneering,' she said, thinking unexpectedly of Hilary Greep and Charlotte M. Yonge, and then again of Archie. She now moved around in a state of incandescent anger. A Mrs Wattle, from Taunton's Social Services Department, had made an appointment to come to see Archie. She was very businesslike on the telephone. Portia thought that she could detect a hard time in the offing. She made a Madeira cake, beating it unnecessarily hard, for tea. Friends in the neighbourhood rang. They were sympathetic and indignant on Portia's behalf. Portia hated it. She rang her daughters. They were also sympathetic and offered to have Archie to stay for a while, but she could hardly send Archie away while he was being investigated. It was possible that in future she would have to get permission for him to travel.

Mrs Wattle turned out to be an infant of about twenty-six. She explained that Archie's behaviour was a temporary aberration and would pass as the illness progressed. 'I think we must consider putting him on medication and having a carer for him. He's getting to be a bit of a handful, don't you think?'

'What kind of medication?'

'The kind that will have him nodding all day in a chair,' Anna said.

161

'He will get worse,' Mrs Wattle explained. 'We need to plan ahead. He's obviously very physically active at the moment and you are no longer young, Mrs Sheldon. We cannot allow a repetition of this sort to occur.' She ate some Madeira cake.

It was ridiculous, Portia thought, to be lectured by someone so young with so little experience of life. She thought of telling her that she had been a magistrate for twenty years and had dealt with many such cases as Archie's. She thought of Mr Catchpole's advice and restrained herself. Anna had no such inhibitions.

'Mummy was a magistrate for years and years. A very wise and humane one, weren't you, darling?' she said.

'Things have changed since Mrs Sheldon was a magistrate. Child abuse is taken rather more seriously now,' Mrs Wattle said.

Portia's cheeks stung with angry heat. What Archie had done was not child abuse. It was abuse of the term to call it that. 'Would you like some more cake,' she asked, holding the knife poised over it, her voice more sweetly vague than ever.

'I won't, thank you,' Mrs Wattle said, 'although it was delicious.'

No rumour about Portia's tribulations ruffled the even rhythm of Katherine's life. She walked her Pekinese, thought of little else than the disposal of Hilary Greep, took some flowers round to Blanche Chambers' bedside in the Royal Free Hospital, and visited Annabel.

Annabel was deteriorating fast. Her room was kept sweatily hot as she lay propped up with a single sheet pulled down to her waist.

Nowadays she could no longer bear even a nightdress to touch her, and so lay vulnerable to the gaze of her women friends. Her flesh hung down in folds. She no longer received men. Her nurses were sweet.

Dust to Dust, Katherine thought looking at her. So soon. Dust to Dust. About once a year Katherine did a detailed examination of her naked body, staring at it in her full-length bathroom mirror, looking for the changes the year had wrought. The rest of the time she avoided looking at herself unless fully clothed with her face ready to be decked out and softened by make-up. She could hardly bear looking at Annabel, but she did look all the same, directly at her. Good manners and affection demanded it. Sometimes Annabel's mind seemed fogged. Once, when Katherine had rung her she had made no sense at all. Katherine had felt shock waves passing up her back to her head. She always felt very threatened by the irrational. It was, after all, the only connection one person has with another. Today Annabel's mind was engaged and interested. Katherine told her about Annabel Bennet's funeral and about George Willborough's 'Heil Hitler'.

'I would have liked to have gone. Of course I couldn't. Looking back, it seems so odd to think of the emotions that propelled one so violently in life. I think in retrospect that it was more a desire to disengage from my own marriage than passion for Annabel's husband. I was *so* bored. Being bored is much more painful than actual pain. Almost any other kind of feeling is preferable to it. I even took up hunting, which I hated. It terrified me. I never felt in control of the horse, especially when it went downhill, and then there were all those branches coming at one. I was sure the horse deliberately went under them, trying to knock me off. But at least in my terror and discomfort I was not bored. Then there was the relief of getting off the horse. The bliss of the bath and the hunger for food. Falling in love with Leonard saved me from all that. It was a much more pleasant way of overcoming boredom, don't you think?'

'Undoubtedly,' Katherine said.

'I didn't give a fig about all those children of Annabel's, and had no intention of taking them on. I had my own children to fight about. I couldn't see why Annabel couldn't look after them. They should have been a consolation to her. It was my refusal to interest myself in his children that made everything fall apart with Leonard. But he did all right in the end, didn't he? Even had more children. But he deserted me. It put me in an impossible position for some time. Although I suppose I'm grateful to him. It got me out of my marriage. I'm not a very nice person. When I allow myself to think about it, even I am shocked by my younger self.'

'It goes the other way round with me. I've become much less nice as I've become older. Particularly since Kenneth died. Living on one's own makes one more selfish and cranky. One no longer thinks one should have to put up with things. There is no longer any point in putting up with things.' Katherine closed her mouth, locking her teeth, in case she continued like a silly rippling brook and said the things she did not wish to say to Annabel. Recently she sometimes found herself saying things without conscious volition.

'I'm wondering about having a clergyman round. Do people?'

'I don't know. Kenneth didn't.'

'What would I say to a reverend if one came round?'

'I suppose you would talk about God.'

'You mean, I would say something like, "I don't know if

164

I believe in an afterlife," and he would say something like, "Don't worry, there is one," and I would say, "Thank you, that's nice to know," and then what would happen?'

'I don't know,' Katherine said again, and then making an effort she said, 'I expect he would enquire about your illness, say a few prayers with you, possibly even offer to bring you communion. Would you like that?'

'I don't know. It might be nice. Dying should be marked in some way, don't you think?'

'Would you like me to contact your local church?'

'I don't know.'

Chapter Twelve

Laura cleaned Maisy's flat for the visit of her mother's friends. At least she cleaned the hall passageway, sitting-room, dining-room and the bathroom. The bedrooms, off limits to the guests, were left in their usual state. Nothing, of course, could be done about the sunken chairs, the rugs with holes in them, the ragged (but original) Morris throw covers turned into curtains, the clutter of books, the papers and ornaments which hardly shifted from year to year, or the inadequate electric fires which in winter made many of Maisy's friends don mittens. The flat was, however, aired and the dust driven out. Maisy did not notice the dilapidation around her. No redecoration had taken place since her husband died. It had been David who had noticed when something needed mending, or if a damp patch appeared on a wall, or if the springs of a chair were collapsing. Maisy had no visual sense and, in any case, thought it absurd to care about such things. But Laura did, a little.

Laura wore slacks below a long shirt to greet them. Moira thought she looked very fetching. She had always liked that gamine look – all eyes – and then there was that mouth! She wondered why Laura had not married.

The three women had dressed for each other. Georgina was wearing a peacock-blue silk suit offset by a crimson-and-yellow scarf. Her puckered lips were magenta and her cheeks strongly rouged. Moira wore a long green silk kaftan, with a pattern of Japanesy-style trees. Maisy was in her best black skirt and the shawl that she always wore for evening occasions. Her face was powdered white. They were pleased by the look of themselves as they sat down to dinner.

It was not until coffee, when Laura left them alone, that Moira introduced the subject of Katherine.

'I'm a bit worried about her,' she said.

Moira was relaxed and cheerful. The evening had been jolly, almost cosy, and Laura had cooked a really very delicious meal, a mixture of brains and sweetbreads in a delicate sauce followed by bananas cooked in rum and brown sugar. Moira had been in heaven.

Georgina was not happy. The conversation buzzed around her. She tried to concentrate but it was difficult with the constriction in her chest. What was she going to do about Georgio? What was the most dignified thing to do? Could she forgive him? It would take years for the anger to die. She didn't have years. As always when she said in her head, 'Get out,' she saw the house empty and herself alone and cold. She would look a fool, an old fool taken for a ride, if she threw him out after discovering how he had diddled her. She practised a way of casually mentioning Georgio's wife and family as though she had always known about them. That might be best. She saw Georgio's wife as a plump peasant stirring a pot with a large spoon. Perhaps the thing would be to call on her? Simply not discuss it with Georgio. Take a cheque – ten thousand was too much, seven would do – and give it to the mother for the boy. Take command. Refuse to be the victim of the story.

Maisy was also paying little attention to the conversation. Her narrow mouth was turned down. Nobody seemed to notice how disgruntled she was feeling. She had watched Georgina and Moira wolfing down all those disgusting brains and sheep's innards in silent rage. She had been unable to get it past her lips. Her crossness had led her to sit silent while the other three had discussed Dada and Peggy Guggenheim. She considered the meal to be one of Laura's little games, presenting a picture of domestic sweetness and light while starving her mother.

'It is not as though we don't all feel strongly about what the wretched girl is saying about Charlotte M. Yonge. Of course we do, and of course Katherine is right to want to stop her. The Pearls *should* protest when her life is fictionalised, and we should do anything legally possible to protect her reputation, but Katherine must be stopped from harming her,' Moira said.

'The law doesn't protect the dead or the elderly,' Georgina said. 'For example, how would Maisy feel if the correspondence David published between himself and Auden, after Auden's death, was used by an unscrupulous biographer to claim that the two of them had been having an affair throughout her marriage?'

'I expect my son would send a letter of protest to the *Guardian*,' Maisy said.

'Much good that would do you and David.'

'What letters?' Moira asked, her voice rising. 'When were they published? How could I have missed them?'

'I can't think. David published them under the title *The Amazing Friendship* and they were serialised in the *Sunday*

Times. David was at a prep school called Down School in Herefordshire when Auden was teaching there. Auden took a shine to him,' Georgina said.

'He was very beautiful,' Maisy said proudly. 'I'll get Laura to get the photograph albums. They corresponded for years. All the time David was at Lancing and later at Oxford, they remained very good friends.'

'How could I have missed it,' Moira wailed. Then unable to resist, in a calmer, happier voice added, 'Though, of course, my special friendship with Auden was at a later date, 1958, when he was living in a cottage outside Salzburg. I was doing some research there. His lover Chester Kallman went away for a few weeks, leaving him on his own. I was still at an impressionable age at the time. It sort of built up. Propinquity, I suspect.'

'My dear Moira, you must have been nearly fifty in 1958,' Maisy said drily.

'I certainly didn't feel it. Wystan was so stimulating that I felt like a student in his presence! We continued our affair in New York some time later.' Changing the subject before Maisy's jealous and sarcastic tongue could probe any deeper, she added to Georgina, 'You seem to be taking Katherine's part.'

'I'm not, exactly.' Turning to Maisy she asked, 'But, Maisy, could you truthfully say that you would not be delighted if someone shot an impertinent biographer who completely distorted your and David's life together?'

'Katherine can't be allowed to shoot Hilary Greep,' Moira said, not liking the near complicity that was developing between Maisy and Georgina. 'Why are you changing your tune?'

'I think,' Georgina said judiciously, 'it's because one

becomes so powerless as one gets old. Everybody is harrying you so. They think they can do anything to you; bundle you into a flat with a lift, blackmail you.' She stopped.

'Why should we be powerless because we are old?' Maisy said, taking up the refrain. 'Why should we be humiliated?'

'What has any of this got to do with Katherine's wish to murder Hilary Greep?' asked Moira, bewildered.

'Nothing,' Maisy said glumly.

'Nothing,' Georgina repeated, 'and of course she isn't going to murder anybody; she's much more likely to delegate the task to one of us. She has always been very good at delegating.'

'Well, I'm not going to do it,' Moira said firmly. 'I'm returning to Saint-Barthélemy.'

'Of course you aren't going to do it. None of us are,' Maisy said crossly. 'We are here to discuss what we are going to do about Katherine. It must be senility!'

'Katherine is not the only one showing signs of dementia. Have you heard Grace is hiring a student to visit Robert two hours a day and read him the *Financial Times* and the *Wall Street Journal*?' Georgina said, who had heard it from Katherine, who had bumped into Grace in the florist at Notting Hill Gate. 'She told Katherine that she thinks Robert is showing signs of understanding what is going on around him.'

'What signs?' Maisy's tone was supercilious.

Now and then Georgina wondered what was happening to Maisy. In recent months she had become crabby and unkind. Formerly she had been only a little sharp and vague. Now there was an undertow to the things she said.

'She didn't specify. She said it was a feeling she had.'

'Grace and her feelings!'

Moira returned to the subject at hand. 'I think we should talk to Annabel about it. I know she's dying and shouldn't be worried, but Katherine wouldn't like to upset her, and if something happened to Hilary Greep after we told her about Katherine's aberration, she *would* be very upset. At least, I think she would,' she added in a more tentative voice. 'I really don't know Annabel very well.'

'When it comes to things like murder, unless there is a known history of violence, I don't suppose anyone knows anyone that well,' Maisy said, thinking of the bruise on her thigh inflicted by Laura that morning when towelling her dry after her bath.

'We mustn't worry Annabel,' Georgina said firmly. 'That would be criminal.'

The telephone rang. It was Katherine. 'Maisy, Blanche has died.'

Blanche's funeral took place in the village of Upton in Buckinghamshire. Her family, who had loved her, were dry-eyed. Her coma had been too long-drawn-out to regret her death. It was a gusty June day with a strong blue sky contending against dirty white cloud. When the sun disappeared the mourners shivered in their cotton clothes. The village was pretty and the graveyard of the Victorian church was picturesquely placed to the north of the village green. Blanche and her husband had weekended for thirty years in a modern bungalow in the neighbouring village of Stockton. As Grace threw a handful of dust into the open grave there were tears in her eyes. It could have been the wind because her eyes watered easily, but as she and Georgina tottered together off the grassy verge, she said, 'I'm a murderer.'

'Not yet,' Georgina said soothingly.

'I told Blanche about the plan to murder Cherry Blossom.'

She must be going gaga, Georgina thought. 'She couldn't possibly have understood.'

'Yes, she did. She died.' Grace wept.

'Why did you do it?'

'I thought a miracle might occur and how wonderful that would be, and that I would have been responsible. Blanche is such a good woman. I thought she might rise from her bed in outrage. You know, take up her bed and come out and castigate us. I thought I might break through the fog around her. That God might help. He can't want us to murder poor little Cherry. I never believe nurses when they say that stroke victims don't understand. I know Robert understands. I had proof of it.'

Grace did not explain to Georgina how she knew. If she told her, Georgina would be bound to tell everyone.

'But what made you think we were going to murder Hilary Greep? We've hardly discussed it.' Georgina was bewildered.

'Katherine told me she had discussed it with you, and that you had a splendid plan, much quicker than her own. In your plan, Hilary would not have time to feel any pain.' She started crying again. 'And now I have murdered Blanche!'

'It's all right, Grace. Even if she did hear you, and even if she did die from shock, it was a happy release. If I ever have a stroke I would love to be startled to death. What a way to go!'

Grace wiped her eyes.

'Mind you,' Georgina said severely, 'you mustn't go worrying Annabel about our frivolous discussions. She

172

hasn't got long now and she shouldn't be worried about what we are getting up to, or not getting up to. In fact it would probably be best if you don't visit her.'

'I don't want to visit Annabel, we've never been close.'

They were joined by Katherine who unlike everybody else looked comfortable in a thin wool black coat and sensible tie-up shoes. 'Maisy wants me to push her back to the bungalow and drink sherry with Blanche's family. I haven't really talked to her properly yet, and I think it would be a good opportunity. Have you seen Portia? She's looking very peculiar.'

Portia looked as she felt. Very unhappy. She had decided not to attend the funeral as she could not bear to leave Archie with Mrs Willis. Then, sleepless at five o'clock in the morning, she had decided to go after all, left a note on the kitchen table, and set off in the car at six-thirty. Mrs Willis had moved into Sheldon Hall. Mrs Wattle, the social worker, had won her point. If they were not to bring Mr Sheldon to court, she said, they had to institute a procedure which would make it impossible for him to wander off again. There must be a resident carer at the Hall. Portia had tried to get round the problem. She suggested that if someone were to come for five hours a day, she would be able to manage perfectly well. Mrs Wattle had been adamant. Gently, she said that someone of Portia's age should be taking it easy rather than running a large house and looking after a man who was physically spry but without the mental capacity to go with it. There was always the risk that Archie would escape to the village and expose himself again. She had hinted that the only reason this crisis had not occurred earlier was that most of the villagers were tenants of the Hall and had not dared to complain about Mr Sheldon's behaviour. There had been mutterings about the Sheldons treating the village as their private fiefdom. Portia felt humiliated. The village and the villagers had become her enemy. She no longer liked to go among them talking of drainage, of leaking roofs, of Mrs Moore's bowel operation, of little Johnny Coggins's deafness and what time old Mr Tebbit would like his weekly lift to the doctor. Fiefdom indeed! A worse blow was to follow. She had intended to sell one of the outlying cottages near the sea and to use the money to hire nice Australian girls from a nursing agency who would be switched every fortnight. She thought this preferable to having one woman with whom she would have to live day in, day out and might come to hate. Then her children started talking about Mrs Willis. They could not understand her reluctance to employ her. Their father liked her and she would be a great deal less expensive than an agency helper. Also, Mrs Willis lived locally, had friends, and would be more self-sufficient than a strange woman. In fact, they could probably avoid selling a cottage if they used her. She gave in. She could think of no reasonable objection to hiring her other than that she did not like her very much. Then Dr Catchpole prescribed tranquillisers for her to give to Archie. Portia flushed each day's supply down the lavatory. If Mrs Wattle checked on her, the right number of pills would be in the bottle. Meanwhile Archie had the freedom of his agility.

After Mrs Willis had been at the Hall for a week, Portia could hardly contain her dislike. She had completely taken over Archie, fussing over him, cooking him boiled eggs with bread soldiers at odd hours just as though he were four years old. She would take him for walks down to the farm to pat the horses or get him to weed, hovering all the while to make sure he did not pull up the plants. It could not last but while it did it was horrible for Portia. All this was being done to free her, but now that she no longer went down to the village, and now that her pleasure in gardening had been destroyed by the proximity of Archie and Mrs Willis communing over the weeds – it was worse than having a radio on – she felt disorientated and dysfunctional. She wandered around the estate fiddling with things. She had accepted invitations for lunch as far away as Barnstaple in the hope of distraction but had been unable to relax. At the thought of Archie and Mrs Willis roaming around the Hall together, probably playing hide-and-seek and peek-a-boo, she felt a violent anxiety. This was what she was feeling now as she drank sherry in Blanche's plain and serviceable bungalow.

'Portia,' Katherine said, looking distracted, 'Maisy wants to go to the loo. That's really more your line. Don't you do charity work in a hospital? Or perhaps that's Grace. Grace will help you. I'll get her.'

Portia and Grace escorted Maisy to the bathroom. Neither of her children had accompanied her to the funeral. The Pearls had managed Maisy's travel arrangements among themselves. Portia was grateful that Blanche's home was a bungalow and they didn't have to manhandle her upstairs. It needed the two of them to get Maisy out of her wheelchair and hold her as she strove to get her knickers down and then lower her on to the lavatory.

'What do you think?' Maisy asked as she sat there. 'Katherine really seems to think we have settled to the idea that we are going to get rid of Hilary Greep.'

'What?' Portia said sharply.

'She thinks it should be death in the London Library, Suddenly, This Summer, when it is quite empty.'

'Oh dear!' Grace said, wringing her hands. 'She did say

something about it to me. But we aren't going to do it, are we?'

'Of course not,' Portia said.

'It does have a rather appealing ring to it: Death in the London Library. Poetic justice. I like the idea of you all chasing her around the stacks brandishing knives! Not that I can help. I'm in a wheelchair.' Maisy added, 'I'm finished, if you could help me up.'

Pulling Maisy's knickers up was a more cumbersome operation than getting them down. It was a relief when they had her settled back in her chair.

'How's Archie?' Grace asked as they wheeled Maisy back to the party.

Portia could not trust her voice and so said nothing.

'How's Archie?' asked Katherine twenty minutes later, breaking her rule never to mention the man's name. She was worried by the visible astrayness of Portia's appearance. If the trouble did not lie with Archie it must be one of the children.

'Not too well,' Portia said.

'In what way not too well? He can hardly be more absent-minded than before?'

'I've had to have someone live in to help look after him.'

'He's not developed dementia; he's not attacked you, has he?'

'No. He wouldn't hurt a fly,' said Portia fiercely. 'Only others don't realise that.'

'Your children have made you get in a helper?'

'No, it's the social services. They say I'm too old to manage him any longer, so there's this ghastly woman who speaks baby talk to him and calls me "Mummy". She says things to Archie like, "I'm sure Mummy would like you to tidy your

176

plate away," and Archie obediently puts away his plate. I hate it. I can't bear it.' Portia was shaking. She finished her sherry in a couple of gulps and put down her glass. 'I must go. It's a long drive.'

'Don't. I hate seeing you so woebegone. Let this Mummy person look after Archie tonight and come home with me. We'll put our feet up and think of something entirely different.'

'Like murdering Hilary Greep?' Portia tried to smile.

'Hush. Do come.' Katherine tapped her with two fingers on her back. 'It will be nice for you to shake off all those Sheldon Hall cares for a night, and it will give me real pleasure. We haven't properly seen each other for ages and ages.'

Unexpectedly Portia said, 'Yes, all right,' and suddenly found herself filled with shaky gladness.

Blanche's funeral had been a long day. Grace was too exhausted to visit Robert in hospital that evening. She went in the following morning at eleven o'clock. Since she was now convinced that Robert was aware of what went on around him, she had taken to bringing flowers and had put photographs of their daughters and grandchildren on the trolley-like thing that went alongside his bed. She explained her absence and told him about Blanche's funeral and about Maisy's fantasy of the Pearls chasing Hilary Greep around the stacks in the London Library. With a guilty shiver of pleasure she felt Robert's reaction to her words as his penis shot upwards between her fingers. She wondered whether in order to retain his interest she would be expected actually to *kill* Cherry Blossom? If, God forbid, they were actually to kill her how was she to entertain Robert after that? What was she *thinking*! She began to wonder about Robert and their life together. Was it normal for a man to get such a charge from the thought of a group of elderly women killing a young girl? He might have been a bit impatient; certainly he had not listened to her when she was telling him something; nor had he consulted her as much as he should have. There had been sexual difficulties sometimes for which he had blamed her, but he had never shown any really sadistic tendencies. Now, here he was revelling in the possibility that the Pearls were going to murder a girl he had never even met. Had he perhaps had a secret life about which she had known nothing? Clubs, whips, snuff movies, call girls? No, not Robert, she said firmly to herself. She remembered him suddenly and with a violent vividness, sitting up in bed beside her, wearing his half-moon spectacles and reading that life of Mountbatten which had been all the rage. Oh Robert, she thought, how we are changed.

Moira booked her fare to Saint-Barthélemy. She didn't like the way things were shaping up. Blanche's funeral, as well as giving her a dreadful wheezy cold in her chest, had made her feel very uneasy. She was dreading the flight as it meant two changes, first at Paris and then at Guadeloupe. She was, she thought, getting too old for such long journeys. Next year she would stay put in Saint-Barthélemy. Her friends were becoming a little strange – not wearing well. She had three days to settle her affairs and then she would be off.

Moira liked to pack over the course of a week. She enjoyed the sight of her large suitcase open in her bedroom and the gradual amassing of dresses, underclothes, shoes, useful things she had picked up in Boots and Peter Jones, and presents for her friends back in Saint-Barthélemy in nicely wrapped packages. She liked taking things in and out and rearranging them to make a smoother pattern. She particularly liked folding her dresses, skirts and blouses so that they fitted neatly the angles of the case. This time she felt crowded by the three days at her disposal, and she was unwell. Her voice disappeared into the rumble in her chest and she breathed with difficulty. She found crème de menthe helped best in clearing the nasal passages, but she was not sure whether it might not be responsible for the dizziness which made it more comfortable to lie on her bed than try to finish her packing. On Monday morning she was to have flown from Heathrow, but when her cleaner arrived in the afternoon to set the flat in order, she found her still there. As Mrs Green changed her shoes to the slippers she kept handy in the kitchen cupboard for cleaning purposes, she heard a faint wheezing coming from the bedroom. 'Hello,' she called. The wheezing became louder as she approached the door. Moira was still in bed in her pink lace nightdress. Her eyes were half open but the irises turned up within the lids. She did not look conscious. Mrs Green called an ambulance.

It was three days before any of her friends found out that Moira was in hospital with bronchial pneumonia. Katherine discovered what had happened. Ringing, and getting no answer, she thought Moira must have absconded to Saint-Barthélemy so she rang her there. Her maid told her that they had been expecting her, but she had not arrived. A car had gone to meet her at the air strip but she had not got off the plane.

Alarmed, Katherine decided to call round on her way to the London Library. Bundling all her Pekinese into a taxi, she asked the driver to wait while she made enquiries at Moira's mansion block. Ringing a neighbour's bell, she learned about the ambulance. The neighbour did not know what hospital

Miss Lockheart had been taken to. 'In the old days it would have been University College Hospital but goodness knows what happens to people now,' she said before cutting off communication with Katherine on the steps.

Moira was in the London Hospital. It was a horrible place, her friends agreed on the telephone, shocked by their odyssey into the East End. Moira was in a large mixed ward with no more than a foot between the beds. There was a lot of noise, odd shouts, grunts, groans and radios playing. Woebegone, Moira was pathetically pleased to see her friends.

'They are supposed to ask you if you mind being in a mixed ward,' she told Grace, the first to visit. Grace brought grapes and smoked salmon with her. Tears came into Moira's eyes when she saw the food.

'You have no idea what it is like,' she told Grace in a whisper. 'I've lost a stone.' She wept as she ate a grape. 'I wish I was in Saint-Barthélemy.'

Grace felt her eyes fill with tears of sympathy. 'It's terrible here, terrible, I agree. We must get you out.' Her alarmed gaze took in the full squalor of the ward. 'We should try to get you into the Royal Free. Much nicer than this.'

'I'm not going there; Blanche died there,' Moira said firmly, and became, all at once, dry-eyed.

Moira remained in the hospital for a week and emerged shaky and unwell. She had received a fright. She might have died. She sat up in bed in her flat, receiving visitors and making notes for her future biographer. She was sometimes moved to tears as she assembled the cast of her life. Her friends thought her interest morbid.

Maisy visited her. Her son John steered her with great difficulty into the lift, leaving her for an hour to drink tea with Moira.

'I am glad you are here,' Moira said. 'As a biographer you can advise me how to leave my papers for the best advantage of my biographer.'

'What biographer?' Maisy enquired.

'Well, I thought I would bequeath my papers to Norwich University. You know I come from round there. At one time I thought of leaving them to New Hall, Cambridge as I used to think of it as my spiritual home. But when I wrote to them about it, the Provost said the college was going through so many changes at the moment that it would be reluctant to take them on. She suggested I should donate them to my local university town and that's Norwich. I assume some admirer of my work will write my biography, but I suppose it could be some academic from Norwich wishing to make his mark. What do you think?'

'Well.' Maisy paused. She did not wish to be brutal, but how else was she to put it? 'I'm not quite sure why you think anyone will want to write your biography, Moira. Most writers don't get written about. And although, of course, you are very good and very popular, you are not really a literary writer.'

'Daphne du Maurier, Georgette Heyer, Agatha Christie, even Margery Allingham have all had biographies written about them.'

'Daphne du Maurier turned out to have led rather a peculiar life, Agatha Christie possibly set up her first husband for murder, Margery Allingham had an unhappy marriage which at least gives some drama. Only Georgette Heyer had a fairly featureless life, although she was very, very popular – and goodness, was her life a bore to read about.'

'I'm just as popular as she was.'

Maisy opened her mouth to reply but thought better of it.

'And my life hasn't been featureless. I have had an amazing life. I've known famous and brilliant people and have had some very interesting romances.'

'Such as Auden.'

'Yes, such as Auden.'

'What's more,' Moira went on crossly, 'I know exactly what my biographer will look like. He will be twenty-eight, tall, dark, with slightly long, swept-back hair, large, heavy glasses, blue eyes, and the suggestion of a three o'clock shadow on his chin. He will be exceedingly clever and he will admire me extravagantly.'

Maisy laughed and said, 'You really do have it all worked out, don't you?'

Moira relaxed and smiled back. 'Do you really think there is a danger that nobody will write my biography?'

'Oh, I don't know. But I wouldn't say it was a certainty. I do think you are taking it all a little too seriously, and I don't think you are dying. I certainly think you will outlive Georgina and me, and probably Grace, who might well have an accident one day. What do you think?'

Chapter Thirteen

Annabel was dying. She had slipped into a light coma. Unable to cry, Katherine moved restlessly around her flat as though the constant movement might expel her misery. She had stopped visiting. There were those who had a closer claim on Annabel's last hours. She did not pray, but she went and lit a candle in a Roman Catholic church and then blew it out again. She wanted to blow out all the other candles too, all those flickering brave attempts to change the ordained chain of circumstances that held human life captive. But she did not. She was no vandal. When she struck, it would be as a snake strikes. Even as she was thinking this, she was aware of her loneliness. In her frailty she sat at the back of the church and wept. Her anger and humiliation were made worse when an arm reached across her shoulders and a woman, smelling faintly of fried onions, asked if she could help her.

Annabel died at nine-thirty that evening. The nurse, who had Katherine's telephone number on a list of those to ring, gave her the news. Katherine asked who had been with her. The answer was: nobody. Her daughter, Mrs Duffle, was now on her way. Katherine felt bitter. As it was summer, the heating was off in her flat and she felt cold. Reaching out for comfort she allowed Rossetti, M. Yonge, Browning, Brahms and Mozart on to her bed. Usually they snuffled and snored in two large dog baskets at the end of her bed. Now, even the company of her dogs failed to console her. When she died she would be alone. For herself she wished for no company, but she would have liked to have been with Annabel as Annabel's last hours drained away. She heard the faint tick of her alarm clock, the friend with whom she had risen rigorously at seven o'clock for the last fifty years. Tomorrow, as usual, she would rise to its call to do less and less. She felt in her own flesh the warmth draining from Annabel's body.

The next morning she felt ill and shaky. Her legs and arms would not do what she asked them to and shivers pricked her skin where her clothes touched her. Her eyes were dazed. A glass pane seemed to separate her from familiar surroundings. Coffee helped. Then, against all her principles, she returned to bed in the afternoon and slept.

The announcement of Annabel's death was in Saturday's *Times*. Georgina was the first to ring her.

'You knew, of course,' she said.

'Yes. Her nurse rang me.'

'Poor Annabel. Poor us. We're dwindling fast.'

Katherine nearly said she could not wait to go, but stopped herself. It would not do.

'They've asked for no flowers but to give a donation to the Macmillan nurses. I wonder how many people who would have sent flowers will do that,' Georgina said.

'I will.'

'And I will. I wonder if Moira will?'

Moira told Georgina that she was not well enough to go to the funeral. There would be no more funerals in the foreseeable future. The last one had nearly killed her; she wasn't going to risk it again. She would think of Annabel there in her flat.

Katherine rang to say she would pick her up in a taxi. 'It isn't far, only to Chelsea. They are burning her so we won't be going on. It's time you went out. You'll become susceptible to germs if you stay indoors much longer.'

'I'm still not well.'

'You're not ill. If you don't get used to going out again, the aeroplane to Saint-Barthélemy will kill you off with all that recycled air.'

Moira decided to go.

It was a social funeral. Annabel's acquaintance had been large. Living singly, she had had friendships that embraced more than one generation. Her great grandchildren's tears made mourning real for the others. Afterwards, an uneasy line-up of her three children and their consorts shook hands and embraced where appropriate, and then everyone dispersed into the lunchtime crowds on the King's Road.

Georgina invited the Pearls back for a drink and sandwiches. She asked Grace who had better legs than she to purchase the sandwiches. Grace, not liking the queues outside the sandwich bars, took a taxi to Harrods food hall where things were nearly as bad. She felt bewildered and battered by the milling scene, and when she arrived forty minutes later at Georgina's house in Belgrave Square she brought with her an oddly inappropriate assortment of things for the Pearls' consumption – fresh lychees, sausage rolls, and some Turkish pastries.

They sat downstairs in the ballroom because it would have been impossible to hoist Maisy up the stairs. The sun hardly glanced in on them and Moira, feeling the gloom as a shudder on her shoulders, clutched her cashmere

185

shawl. All were unusually aware of the gaseous smell of dry rot.

'She has a voice that would give pleasure as the speaking clock,' Katherine said to herself, as she unpacked flaky baklava from the carrier bag Grace had left on the coffee table. There had to be some point to Grace.

Unable to face the thick wads of sweet pastry or the sausage rolls, the Pearls concentrated on Georgina's Cyprus sherry.

'I don't quite know why, as neither Blanche nor the two Annabels had been active Pearls in the last year or so, but going to all these funerals makes one feel that the Pearls are greatly diminished,' Maisy said.

'I think quite soon each of us will be put under a tea cosy, placed by a television set and left,' Georgina said.

'Not Katherine,' Portia said gently.

'What?'

'Not Katherine,' Maisy repeated in a loud, sharp voice.

'No, not Katherine. She will be locked up in Holloway Prison and Percy will visit her on Thursdays,' Georgina said.

'Where *is* Percy?' Katherine asked, suddenly aware of unusual signs of neglect in the house.

'I think she must have found a man. She hasn't been around for a week or two, but she rang me up at ten in the evening the other day from a call box in a pub to abuse me. That's always a sign.'

'She doesn't ring and abuse me,' Katherine said.

'But then she doesn't think you owe her. She has always believed me to be in her debt since I came here as a bride. She thinks she is an old retainer and so has the privilege of abuse. She reads too many cheap novels.'

'How's Georgio?' Katherine asked. There was something

186

missing from the house and it was not just Percy's slatternly touch.

'I don't suppose he's any different than usual. Certainly not ready for a tea cosy yet.'

Georgina had decided that there was no reason why anyone should ever know about her difficulty with Georgio. It was not as though she and Georgio went out much together. His presence or non-presence in the house could simply be fudged, especially to Christopher. In fact, it was very important that it *should* be fudged to Christopher. Without the fixture of a man in her life, a woman was treated like a cracked vase, to be put away at the back of a cupboard or boarded up in an apartment with only a lift as lifeline to life. A few days ago – in fact, the day of Annabel's final coma – she had had her hair bounced into tight curls, dressed herself in her pink silk suit and ordered a taxi to take her to Stockwell. In her handbag was a cheque for six thousand pounds for the mother of Georgio's children. (On reflection, seven thousand pounds had seemed an unnecessarily large amount.) She had waited for the taxi, sitting on a hard, upright chair in the hall. When the bell rang she had been unable to move, clutching at her bag, her mind unfocused. What she could not picture was ringing the doorbell on the second floor of some council estate, waiting for the door to open, and then stepping forward into . . . what? Age meeting youth? What dignity was there in that? The second peal of the door forced her uncomfortably to her feet. She knew she was not going. Instead, she asked the milkman to post the cheque for her.

Katherine's voice brought her back to the present. 'Moira is clutching her shawl as though she wishes it *were* a tea cosy.'

Moira pretended to relax. 'I'm not used to the weather here. I should be in Saint-Barthélemy.'

'You will be soon,' Katherine promised.

'Ah,' Moira sighed, sudden terror causing her insides to lurch. It was, of course, only a fantasy, but as she lay awake, depressed and lumpen in her bed, thinking of her end, she had wondered how the orchestrated death of Hilary Greep by the Pearls might affect the chances of her biography being written by the young man in glasses. She would, of course, have to place a moratorium of twenty-five years on her papers, to make sure all the Pearls were dead. This would inevitably mean a delay in the writing of the biography – or maybe, she thought as her optimism rose, a second biography at some later date, the first biographer being perfectly content to highlight the affair with Auden. But what if Maisy were right? What if she were not still in print twenty-five years after her death? Would it then occur to the young academic to investigate her life?

Looking around at the others she could not deny that they looked anything but hearty. Would a ten-year embargo on her papers not see them all through? At Blanche's funeral she had noticed that Portia had suddenly seemed shrunken, while Georgina looked ghastly under her rouge. Surely ten years would do? Of course, if she turned out to be more robust than the others, she might get away with only a five-year moratorium after her death – or even none if she survived them all.

'I know, it's rather a gloomy subject, but I do think we should deal with it,' Katherine said benignly. 'We have Georgina to thank for a rather good suggestion to settle the matter.'

'It was a joke,' Georgina said, looking exceedingly uneasy. 'I was just playing "if". Katherine's suggestion was so particularly gruesome.'

188

'What was Katherine's idea?' Maisy asked.

'I thought that we couldn't do better than go to the maestro of suspense, Alfred Hitchcock. It seemed to me appropriate that her death should take place in the London Library. It is, after all, in there that we first discovered that literary perfidy was about to be played on the reputation of Charlotte M. Yonge – or rather Moira discovered it for us.'

Moira looked suitably gratified. Thinking of the shortness of the moratorium on her papers, she began to feel quite well and allowed the shawl to slip from her shoulders.

'It has to be admitted, however,' Katherine continued, 'that we are all a little too old for chasing her around the stacks with butcher knives. She is, after all, young and healthy and, I have noticed, does not wear heels on her shoes. I had this vision of her running terrified along the iron-grid passageway near Science and Miscellaneous with her heels becoming stuck in the gaps as she ran, and the more able-bodied of us (myself and Grace) crouched double, riding the wooden book lifts as they creaked slowly up and down, keeping pace with her movements as she clambered about the iron staircases. Meanwhile, Portia and Moira would follow steadily behind her, gradually shepherding her into the Fiction stacks where we would corner her in the section occupied by the works of Charlotte M. Yonge. There we would stab or garrotte her or whatever, and leave her to be discovered at the scene of her crime.'

'What about me? What would I be doing?' Maisy asked.

'You, from your wheelchair, would behave somewhat like a football coach, tracking her movements as she ran this way and that, following the action from below. No amount of crouching and hiding in dark corners in the stacks would be hidden from you. Like a cox directing a crew of a rowing boat you would be able to exhort and direct the Pearls going about their bloody business. But on reflection, I could see that this would be impracticable.

'My second idea, which comes from that master of the Gothic, Poe, would, I think work. He uses it twice, in "The Black Cat" and in "The Cask of Amontillado". In both stories the villainous protagonist walls up his victim in the cellar of his house. In the first, and most terrifying, case the murderer, who has murdered his wife, is undone by nemesis in the form of his pet, a huge black cat whom he accidentally walls up with his wife's body. But it is 'The Cask of Amontillado' which I hoped we might emulate. In it, you will remember, the villain bricks up his victim alive then walks away. My plan is that at closing time on the Friday of the August bank holiday we should lock Miss Greep into that unused small room adjacent to the Fiction stacks, having given her a massive sleeping draught. I thought this could be best effected by Grace inviting her to tea as they seem to have a tea-time relationship. Given the fact that August is the holiday season, there would be a fair chance that her body would not be discovered for a week or two. The advantage of this plan would be that we would not actually be committing murder. We would merely be giving her a sleeping pill and locking her in a room and letting nature take its course.'

'It's completely harebrained. She would probably survive and point the finger at us,' Maisy said.

'It appealed because it would have been a literary death, but Georgina's suggestion is safer and will cause little suffering.'

'Well, what is it?' Maisy asked.

Katherine told them.

Feeling shaky and excited, all of them scuttled home. They had done nothing yet. And of course they *would* do nothing.

Grace found that she burst into tears at unexpected moments. Even the nurses now recognised that there was a change in Robert's condition. There was distinct movement in the fingers of his left hand. Nurse Lacy had said to her only that week, 'He always seems particularly lively after your visit, Mrs Piedmont. You are like a tonic!' Grace had felt stricken. Stricken! As she thought about this she decided that she would write to her daughter Alison in Washington.

Darling Alison [she wrote],

I have such good news. Daddy is showing signs of understanding what is happening around him, possibly because I shocked him by telling him something a bit shocking about The Chaplet of Pearls. You remember that I belong to a group who meet a few times a year to discuss the works of the Victorian writer Charlotte M. Yonge? Recently we discovered that a young girl was writing her life and was going to say the most monstrous and disgusting things about her, things, moreover, which are completely untrue. The Pearls decided that this must not be allowed to happen and somehow a decision seems to have been made to do away with her. Robert seems to like the story of our meetings. Of course, nothing is really going to happen but I am a bit upset.

She stopped writing. How could she say that she sometimes wondered if she should go along with the scheme to stop Robert losing interest? Oh dear, Alison was going to think she was off her head.

She wrote:

Of course, I don't really mean to do anything, even if it is this that is causing Robert's improvement. And of course the others aren't really going to kill her either. I visited Blanche Chambers in hospital, who used to be the spokesman of the Pearls until her stroke, and when I told her she promptly died. Alison, I am worried and lonely. I feel I am quarrelling with your father when I go in and talk about it. Before, I thought in some funny way that we were quite close. Closer in some ways than when he was well. I felt I was contributing something to his welfare. Now, whatever it is I am contributing, I'm not sure I like it. I am reading one of Charlotte M. Yonge's novels called *Nutty's Father*, trying to understand what it is all about. It seems particularly wrong to be fantasising about killing somebody when you don't really understand why you are doing it. The story is about a girl who gives up her youth to look after her horrible father and then marries an elderly manufacturer of umbrellas. It seems very straightforward to me, but this girl says that it shows that Charlotte M. Yonge was sexually abused by her father! We all know that Charlotte M. Yonge was a hard-working Christian spinster much concerned with the moral upbringing of girls. It does seem a shame that this girl is going to say these terrible things about her in print.

Reading this letter makes me realise how ridiculous my unease is. You must think me very silly.

How is William? I expect it is very hot. How are Mary and Douglas? Give them a kiss from Grandma. I miss you all so much, especially you, Alison.

All my love, Mummy

She addressed it and put it into her handbag. Then she thought, what if she fell over in the street on the way to the post-box and her bag was opened to discover who she was, and the letter was read? What then? They would all be in terrible trouble. She took it out and put it on the hall table. And there it stayed.

Sitting on the train to Taunton after the funeral, Portia tried to work out why she was behaving so erratically. She was a believing member of the Church of England. She prayed every night, on her knees, before getting into bed. What kind of a Christian was she? Something was out of kilter in her. She was angry all the time now, and the ripples of satisfaction she sometimes felt were angry ripples. She was angry with her children whenever one of them rang. She didn't say anything but she could feel it on the tip of her tongue. She was impatient at the sound of their voices and no longer interested in their concerns. Harry was coming on his own for the weekend. Perhaps it would break the 'out of kilter' feeling and she would regain her perspective on this whole business of Hilary Greep. Meanwhile, she would re-read *Scenes and Characters*, immerse herself in the world of Charlotte M. Yonge as a crusader might read the Bible before going into battle. There was, she knew, a wickedness in equating the killing of an untruthful biographer with that of a Christian knight killing heathens for Christ's sake. Or was there? The crusaders did some pretty horrible things in the certainty of pleasing God and gaining a place in heaven. Why should striking a blow for what was real and truthful, for integrity in the written word, be any different? Why should Charlotte M. Yonge's real life, thoughts and feelings be distorted for the venal advantage of some sneering, smug young academic?

She found herself shaking with anger.

Harry arrived on the cheap train which left Paddington after six o'clock. This meant a late dinner. Mrs Willis had fed herself and Archie earlier. They were both now sitting uncomfortably in the ground-floor sitting-room watching *Give Us a Laugh* on television, entirely content. Arriving back at the Hall from meeting the train, Portia and Harry could hear the loud, raucous, unnatural laughter emanating from the machine. Portia hoped it sounded as invasive to Harry as it did to her, but said nothing. She had made carrot soup flavoured with coriander, cold salmon with mayonnaise, potato salad, a green salad and a chocolate sponge cake with whipped cream for his supper. She ate, as usual, very little. Harry ate with pleasure and left nothing on his plate to cause his mother distress. The pleasure Portia felt at seeing her tall, blond, well-knit son sitting at ease, eating what she had prepared for him, did not lift her depression. Instead, unexpected tears welled in her eyes. If Harry came home she could use her surplus energy in looking after him. Please God make him tire of London life, she thought.

Harry was only coming for the weekend but he gave promise of how it might be if he did return to run the estate by bringing a suitcase full of dirty washing for her to do. Portia boiled his shirts in a large cauldron on the Aga kept for this purpose. Then she passed them through the old mangle in the scullery. After that she hung the laundry to dry outside the kitchen window. She did have a drier but when the sun was out she thought men's clothes all the fresher for being exposed to country air and sunlight.

Harry was kind to his father. 'Well, Father, how are you, old chap?' he asked on Saturday morning at breakfast. 'How about us going on an inspection of the fields this morning.'

Archie looked at Mrs Willis. 'Does he do the gardening?' he asked.

'He's your son Harry, Mr Sheldon. Come down from London for the weekend to say hello to you.'

'Oh, he's my son,' Archie said with an air of enlightenment.

'Yes, I'm Harry. How about a walk round the fields?'

Archie looked at Mrs Willis.

'That would be fun, wouldn't it, Mr Sheldon?' Mrs Willis said encouragingly.

'Where would you be?'

'I'll be right here having a second cup of tea.'

Archie looked at the strange young man. 'All right,' he said.

They walked in silence. Archie said nothing to the young man walking beside him except occasionally to ask him who he was. Now and then Harry remarked on the trees, the state of the fencing, the grass and even the weather. Archie replied in an interested voice, 'Yes, isn't it.'

During their two-hour absence Portia boiled and cooked and Mrs Willis drank her tea and read the *Daily Express*.

At two o'clock on Sunday afternoon Portia started ironing. She had just finished when Harry left to catch the six-thirty train back to London.

Harry's visit did not alleviate the anxiety that was now Portia's familiar, but she was relieved that she did feel love, almost overwhelming love for him. She hardly felt the full force of his parting remark, 'Mrs Willis seemed a jolly good sort,' until after he had gone. Then she was faced with the actuality of dinner with Archie and 'the jolly good sort'.

Having seen Archie to bed at eleven-thirty and locked the door into the passage so that he would have to pass through her room if he wished to go to the lavatory or for a prohibited wander, she said her prayers, then settled down to reading *Scenes and Characters* until nearly half-past-two.

Georgina heard a noise, a scuffling or tiptoeing on the stairs. In a flash she was out on the landing, without her stick, holding on to the door jamb. Georgio was opening the door to his bedroom.

'Did you think I wouldn't hear you?' she yelled. She looked wild. She had taken off her dress in preparation for bed and was in her slip, with her skimpy hair half in curlers. Her greased face lit up the folds in her skin.

'You needn't shout. I'm not deaf,' Georgio said, turning towards her.

'Yes, you are. You're deafer than I am.'

'Don't be silly. You've got a hearing aid.'

'Exactly. You need one.'

'No, I don't.'

'Yes, you do.'

Georgio opened his mouth and then shut it again.

'Sneaking off to bed. Hoping I wouldn't hear you. Let me tell you, I've been sleeping with my hearing aid in. Don't think that you can use this house just to change your clothes and keep your suitcase.'

'I just wanted to give you time to calm down and get used to the situation. I know it's upsetting. My wife was very angry when I told her that I had fallen in love with this English woman and was going to live with her. Or to be accurate, I had already come to England with you before I wrote and told her. I'm not sure it was not worse for her than for you. She had the children. But she got used to it.'

'I am not some Greek peasant woman.'

'Nor is she.'

'And what about the money I sent her? Has she thanked me? No. Have you thanked me? No. Has your wretched son thanked me? No.'

'It's not enough. You always do things meanly, Georgina. It's late. Too late for all this. Let's talk tomorrow morning.'

'Can't,' Georgina snapped with angry satisfaction. 'Christopher comes tomorrow morning. He's bringing a team of builders.'

'Bother. I tell you what, I'll bring your breakfast up to your bedroom and we will talk together then. Christopher will not come into your bedroom without permission. I am sure we can sort things out between us, Georgina. Try to remember the twenty years we've rubbed along together, not the other.'

'Get me my stick.' As she turned into her room she added sadly, 'I doubt we can sort it out. Christopher wants to put us in a mansion flat with a lift. I don't think we are in any condition to move somewhere else together.' As she spoke she realised the truth of her words and felt despair.

Chapter Fourteen

Friday of the August bank holiday dawned to clear blue skies and the promise of a scorching weekend. Most of those who would leave work early today to avoid the rush-hour exodus felt a lightening of spirits, but not the Pearls, who for the most part had slept little. Portia stayed the night with Georgina. She thought they might soften and weaken in their intent. God in his mercy might save them from disaster. There was little chance of that happening if she stayed with Katherine. Instead, they sat drinking late into the night. Georgina prodigiously, Portia less; a little went a long way with her. Portia hardly noticed the scaffolding inside the house but Percy, after returning briefly, had moved out again, saying it was uninhabitable. Georgina thought she could hold out for another week or two, but the scaffolders were now scratching at her bedroom door. Georgio appeared so rarely that Georgina thought he had decamped. 'He says the dust and grit are ruining his suits,' she explained to Portia.

'All is chaos, decay and death,' Georgina declaimed as she climbed the stairs arm in arm with Portia at two-thirty that night. Georgina slept heavily and snored so loudly that Portia could hear her through the wall. Unable to bear the loneliness of the bright sun shining through the torn fabric of the ragged curtains, Portia brought her tea in bed at seven-thirty. Severely hung-over, Georgina was not grateful.

That night Grace had quite simply wanted to die. She prayed that God would carry her off in her sleep. She dreamed that two birds, a little larger than blackbirds, with exotic striped plumage, swooped down upon her, uttering harsh cries as she walked the narrow labyrinth of streets behind Notting Hill Gate.

In the morning, over breakfast, she thought she would faint from tiredness and hunger. How was she to eat her toast? She wondered what Hilary Greep was having for breakfast on this, the last day of her life. I'll move to the country and never visit Robert again, she thought. I'll kill myself, that is what I'll do. I won't answer the telephone and I'll kill myself.

She drank the tea and threw away the toast.

After breakfast she pottered aimlessly around the house, accidentally breaking things and laboriously sweeping them up. At eleven o'clock Katherine's driver rang the doorbell, and there was Katherine, head poking out of the car door, patting the car seat beside her. Vibrating from the top of her head down to her toes, Grace collapsed into the car. Katherine patted her hand all the way to Baker Street to pick up Moira.

When Katherine and Grace arrived to collect her, Moira was as fresh as a daisy: coiffed, made-up, and wearing a bright frock emblazoned with poppies.

Too bright, Katherine thought. Moira should not draw attention to herself on such a mission.

Moira had worked hard to achieve her summery appearance. She had slept heavily under the influence of a sleeping pill, only to awaken, heart pounding, at five o'clock. Cherry Blossom, pretty, childlike, sweetened by her vulnerability, was before her inward eye. I must banish her, she thought frantically, or I will have a heart attack and die. She imagined herself a twelfth-century crusader going through his knightly ritual before battle. She had written such a scene in the past. Her breath slowed. They were, after all, latter-day knights, going into battle on behalf of Truth and Integrity in the Written Word. They were the knights of Charlotte M. Yonge: her Chaplet of Pearls. They should have their own rituals before battle and she knew exactly what these should be. Rising, she relaxed her sweaty, aching limbs in the hot scented water of a bath, rubbed sweet-smelling oils into her arms, legs and neck. Afterwards, covering her face in a white mud pack, she painfully cut her toenails. This, she thought, is as good as any exercise invented by gym sadists. More enjoyably, she manicured her fingernails, painting them a rosy, shiny pink. Lastly, with a sigh of contentment, she stretched out on the floor with a book supporting her head. Concentrating first on her toes, she then consciously relaxed her legs, hips, rib cage, shoulders and neck until bathed in sleepy well-being. By nine-thirty when she sat down to a breakfast consisting of orange juice, coffee and a croissant she felt ready for anything.

Dressing in the morning was the most painful part of Maisy's day. This slow task was worse on this particular morning because her anger with Laura made her limbs angular and awkward. Laura's touch was hateful to her. The previous evening Laura had gone out and John had come to supper. He told her that they could no longer continue to support her independent life in Hampstead. Laura would no longer look after her, and it was therefore necessary to sell the

200

flat so that there should be enough money to take care of her. This meant she would have to go into a home. He had found a modern, well-conducted home in Acton which would take her in. It was a single-storey building built around a courtyard and had a fountain, tubs of geraniums, and terraces with easy ramps for wheelchairs.

'It is a reasonably priced, half-privatised NHS enterprise. We are lucky to get you in,' he explained. 'And, of course, you will come out to me and Maureen most weekends. We are giving you the children's room in the basement next to the dining-room, so you will only need to move between the ground floor and there. You can have your own furniture, books and things. Of course it's a compromise but surely not so terrible!' he pleaded. 'You will be with us most weekends.' John was lying. It had taken him weeks of negotiation with Maureen to win her consent to his mother staying one weekend a month. Maureen had never liked Maisy and saw no reason to put herself out more than she did already.

'You mean I will travel from Acton to a West Kensington basement and then back to Acton again. Goodness, what excitement!'

'It's no different from travelling between Hampstead and West Kensington.'

'At least I sometimes see my friends in Hampstead. I can hardly receive them in Acton.'

'Mother, you know it can't go on like this between you and Laura.'

'If I can bear it, she can bear it.'

'But *I* can't bear it.'

They looked at each other.

'I can't go on pretending that Laura is not mistreating you.

201

It makes me anxious all the time, and it is turning Laura into a bad woman. That isn't fair to her. If she can't look after you out of love, then she shouldn't be looking after you at all. If it were possible I would have you with us, but it isn't. Maureen has her own interests and I must respect them. The Acton home isn't gloomy. The old people are not crazed and incontinent. The staff are pleasant and the food edible.'

'I won't go. I will manage on my own.'

'You can't and I can't afford a team of nursing help. You have to go. I promise you it will work out.'

Maisy said not another word. She hardly ate the stew although it was the first decent meal Laura had cooked in weeks.

John was nearly in tears when he left. He hated his wife and his mother, detested Laura and could think of nothing good about his sons. He rang his mistress from his car phone. Her husband was at home, but she talked to him for half an hour and made him laugh.

Maisy's thoughts were far from Hilary Greep as Laura struggled with her recalcitrant arms and legs. Laura thought it was like fighting with a fifteen-month-old baby who did not want to co-operate, only her mother was a tough old walrus of eighty-three. Laura badly wanted to be agreeable. After all, she had won. Her mother would never annoy her again. She could be as childishly angry and unpleasant as she liked, but she, Laura, would be a saint of sweetness, a shining example of filial duty.

'If you are to be ready for Georgina and Portia we are going to have to get this on to you.' Laura pulled at the material covering Maisy's head with sharp tugs.

'It's not my fault; you put it over my head crooked,' Maisy

202

said, unaware that the very sinews of her body were lining up with the thoughts in her head.

A van and two muscular men had been hired for the day to take Maisy and her wheelchair to the London Library. The men would lift her wheelchair up and down the steps of the building.

By the time Georgina and Portia arrived with the van to collect her at a quarter-past eleven, Maisy was waiting in her chair, composed and fully dressed. She had hardly given a thought to the business in hand. Only when she saw Portia standing there (Georgina remained in the van) did the reality of what they were about to do enter her mind. Her stomach lurched.

'I need to go to the bathroom,' she said to Laura.

'You've only just been.'

'I can't help it. I need to go.'

In consequence it was nearly twenty to twelve before the van set off again. They were running late, Katherine would be cross but it did not really matter. Nothing mattered until after lunch. Each of them was conscious of that thought.

'What about lunch? We never thought of lunch,' Georgina said.

'I can't say I'm feeling very hungry.' Portia had never felt less hungry in her life.

'That's not the point. If we don't eat we might start doing things wrong. I'm never at my best when I'm hungry. Don't you want something, Maisy?'

'Not now. But if we have to stay there until after two o'clock, I will be feeling very hungry.'

Portia stated the obvious. 'Well, we can't eat. You can't eat in the London Library.'

'We can get some sandwiches on the way and eat them

in the van. There is no point in Maisy getting out of the van until after they have left for the cocktail bar. Hilary might find it a bit odd if all the Pearls are hanging around the London Library at the same time,' Georgina said.

'I can't understand why Katherine insisted we should be there hours before we will be needed,' Portia said.

'She wants to make sure that we all turn up before Moira and Grace start the thing rolling, and I don't blame her. Personally, I feel like turning back,' Maisy said.

'Let's turn back,' Portia urged.

They looked at each other. The other two said nothing and the van drove on.

Darling Cherry [Hilary Greep read],

We are well. I hope you are too and that your work is going well. Things go on much as usual. Your Dad was away on the road two nights last week and he was very tired when he came home. He's not as young as he was. You should think of that sometimes. He's quieter. He doesn't say as much as he used to when you used to visit us. I don't think he would say anything very much except be glad if you came back.

The garden looks nice, though Dad had the cherry trees cut down last week. I miss them. Their absence makes me think about you more than ever. I hope all goes well with you. Any boyfriend? Ann Marsden from your form is getting married next week. Her boyfriend does the electronics for transport in Oxford. Lights and such.

Dad has taken down the third flying duck on the staircase. The wall looks funny with just two! He put

204

the flying duck in the bin but I took it out and hid it in one of my clothes drawers. One day I hope I can put it back!

We miss you ever so much.

Love from your Mum XX

Hilary placed the letter on her desk, and then pushed it quickly off into the wastepaper basket. Since discovering her address her mother wrote to her every week. Letters that said nothing, because her mother did nothing and had nothing of interest to say. She felt uneasy about the letter lying in the wastepaper basket. She rarely threw things out so except for the letter the basket was empty. She took it out again and put it on the edge of the desk, where in all likelihood, she thought, it would fall off of its own volition to join the rest of the stuff on the floor.

She looked around for her black-cloth shoulder bag. The room badly needed cleaning, particularly the cat's litter tray which was over-spilling. She resolved to clean everything up in the evening. Her bag, a little damp, was in the bath. Hilary deeply resented her bag. One day she would liberate herself from it. So far her attempts to do so had ended in disaster. How did men manage, she wondered? As tortoises carry their houses on their back, women take the symbols of their domesticity on their shoulders. Good, she thought, make a note of it, and she did.

She was meeting Moira Lockheart and Grace Piedmont at the London Library at twelve o'clock. Before then she wished to return books and look up some references. She would infinitely have preferred to spend the day at her word processor. The Pearls, she thought, were becoming rather a bore. How dare they investigate her, call on her mother and give her address to her, and why had Grace Piedmont dropped in for tea? They seemed to think they owned Charlotte M. Yonge, and were in charge of her estate. When she had attended their meeting she had thought them rather quaint. No longer; she must make it plain that they could not pursue her and expect her to have lunch and tea with them, have cosy chats about Charlotte and go 'Oho' and 'Haa' about the little snippets of information they dangled in front of her. Probably Moira was lonely. It was said that the elderly often were. Perhaps, once she had finished her work on Charlotte M. Yonge, she should have a kid. She thought of her room filled with all the paraphernalia of babyhood and the baby lying on the bed, and then she thought of the cat and the overflowing litter tray. She stroked the smooth, surface of her word processor with affection; it was the only truly neat thing in the room. She decided to risk the loneliness of old age.

Grace had never liked the London Library. She was not a member and had only been there two or three times before. She had always thought it a spooky place even before Katherine explained the plan to kill Hilary. Now, sitting in the mellow green Reading Room, she thought it sinister. Not at all like the Harrods Lending Library. She had been sad when that closed down.

Katherine had given Grace the *Daily Telegraph* to read while she and Moira went to find books. Any moment Grace expected someone to tap her on the shoulder and ask if she was a member. There was only one other person in the room, a man sitting at the table, scribbling away at something. She tried to concentrate on the front page of the

206

paper. GIRL BATTERED TO DEATH ON PECKHAM COMMON, she read. Her stomach churned. Putting down the paper she rushed to the lavatory. When she returned Portia was standing in the Reading Room looking ill at ease. She seemed relieved to see Grace. 'Where's Katherine?' she whispered.

'In the stacks.' Grace's head vibrated like her washing machine on final spin.

Portia sat her down and took her hand. 'Don't! You don't have to do anything. Go home. Just get up and go home.'

Katherine came through the swing door. She smiled and gave a little wave, and beckoned them out.

'Maisy and Georgina are in the van,' Portia explained. 'Otherwise Hilary might think we are a Greek chorus.'

'That's fine. Here, take these.' Katherine handed two blue pills to the vibrating Grace.

'I can't swallow pills without water.'

Katherine accompanied her to the Ladies'.

On entering the library, Hilary saw Moira and Grace standing by the book counter. Moira waved gaily and Hilary gave a little half-hearted wave back.

'I am afraid I have to return some books and find some others. Do you mind waiting?' she asked.

'Not at all. Why don't you get rid of your books now. You can always pick up your other ones after lunch. We are going to a charming little cocktail bar in King Charles Street. An old haunt of mine. There is a wonderful black barman who mixes and shakes like a dream.'

Grace made a little squeaky noise in the back of her throat.

'I'm not sure I want to drink cocktails in the middle of the day,' Hilary said.

'Nor do I.' Grace was miraculously brave.

'Nonsense, it's my birthday. It's my birthday celebration to myself. I always have cocktails for lunch on my birthday. It's my treat to treat you and Grace.'

'I don't want them,' Hilary said through gritted teeth. She saw any prospect of work in the afternoon disappearing.

'When you see Washington shaking them, you won't be able to resist, either the cocktail or me!' Moira took her hand and squeezed it. Then, taking her arm, she led the way out of the Library. Grace followed behind. They passed the van where Maisy, Georgina, Portia and Katherine were eating egg mayonnaise sandwiches.

Hilary did have a cocktail, and then another, and another, and another. Her first, a Pineapple Rumrunner, which was served out of a scooped-out pineapple, had Bacardi rum, apricot brandy, pineapple juice, orange juice, lemon juice and grenadine. It tasted like the smoothest blend of fruit juices but with the gentlest, warmest kick. During this first drink, which was sucked out of a straw, she tried to explain, on prompting from Moira, how she might approach the job of appraising the work of a writer such as Charlotte M. Yonge. She quoted Roland Barthes. '"We now know that a text is not a line of words releasing a single 'theological' meaning (the message of Author-God) but a multi-dimensional space in which a variety of meanings, none of them original, blend and clash."'

'How interesting!' Moira said, ordering after much discussion a Washington Special for Hilary. This, she explained, was really called a Juiseppe Special, and had apricot brandy, orange juice, pineapple juice and a scoop of pistachio ice-cream. She chose for herself a Manhattan, having started with a White Lady. 'And I suppose what you are doing is blending and clashing Miss Yonge?'

'Yes, I suppose that is what I am doing.' She liked the sound of the phrase. 'I'm blending and clashing Miss Yonge.'

'Making a delicious cocktail of her.'

Hilary laughed. 'Making an absolutely delicious cocktail of her.' After that she had a Handlebar which consisted of Scotch, Drambuie and lime cordial and then lastly a Between the Sheets made of brandy, white rum and Cointreau. They gave high, high pleasure.

Moira kept her company with a Harvey Wallbanger. Grace had a White Lady. It cheered her up.

They did not feel in the least hungry, and at two o'clock, chanting 'Blend and clash', they wobbled their way, holding fast to each other, back to the Library.

Rigid with tension, Portia, Maisy and Georgina watched them mount the steps.

'Three minutes to go,' Maisy said, looking at her watch.

As Moira and Hilary staggered through the Library front door with Grace following behind, Katherine appeared at the end of the hall coming out of the section marked Societies. She started with well-simulated surprise and beamed at them. 'Well, what a surprise! What have the three of you been up to?'

'We've been celebrating my birthday with a drinkie-poo. We've come back to collect books, haven't we, Hilary?'

'Ah, Hilary, that reminds me,' Katherine said. 'I have found something in *Crockford's Clerical Dictionary* which pours considerable and unexpected light on Charlotte M. Yonge's relationship with the Reverend Keble. I have been meaning to drop you a note about it, but as you are here, let me show it to you.'

'*Crockford's* is in the basement. Let's all go down to the

basement,' Moira said gaily, putting out a hand to steady herself on the counter.

Katherine gave her a look to freeze her soul. 'Yes, let's,' she said.

'Yes, let's go and do some blending and clashing in the basement,' Hilary said and giggled.

Moira joined merrily in.

'You are drawing attention to yourself,' Katherine said with quiet fury to Moira. 'You're drunk.'

'Perhaps a little bit tipsy. Don't worry.' She patted her hand. 'Come on.'

Moira led the way to the door to the basement and placing each foot very carefully, with one hand on the wall and the other on the rail, descended the stairs.

As they disappeared down the stairs, the two muscular helpers who had come with the van carried Maisy in her wheelchair to the top of the Library steps. Portia wheeled her in, placing her strategically in the middle of the entrance hall.

'Give me your list, and I will go and look for the books,' she said.

Maisy handed over her list of books. 'You will need to go to the third floor for those two,' she pointed, 'but this one is on the second floor, and those will be on the first.'

'As there are quite a few, perhaps it would be nicer for you to wait in the Reading Room?' Portia suggested.

Seeing Georgina enter the library and make her way, leaning heavily on her stick, towards the stacks at the back, Portia started to push Maisy hurriedly towards the lift, cutting across Georgina's path. They met in heavy collision. Georgina fell across the wheelchair, her stick skidding across the floor. The chair tipped over and, as

Georgina fell, Maisy tumbled on to the floor. Maisy lay spread-eagled, face down, shouting incoherently. Georgina groaned. She had felt something crack.

Portia, meaning it, cried, 'Oh dear! Oh dear!'

Staff came running. People, crossing the hall, came running.

As instructed, although almost by accident, Grace found herself in front of the basement door. 'It is most unlikely that anyone would wish to go to the basement while all that is going on,' Katherine had told her, 'but somebody might try going to the Gents'. If they do, you are to faint.'

Grace did not think it would be at all difficult to faint. She thought she might well faint in any case.

Down in the basement Katherine and Hilary were in the stacks. The basement stacks were unlike the other stacks in the library. Made of metal, they were ten foot high and moved sideways on wheels, opening and closing in the manner of a concertina. Each couple of the twelve stacks was attached to each other and could be opened and closed by the turning of a handle. Some of the largest and heaviest books were kept in them. Katherine and Hilary, back to back, were examining huge bound volumes of *Crockford's* in the fifth and sixth stacks. Katherine said, 'I'm sure it was in this one.' Katherine handed the volume to Hilary, who was hardly able to hold it, and was leaning back heavily against the stack behind her. 'Look at this page and the next page. The trouble is I haven't got the reference on me but I am sure it was the middle volume in the fifth row of the fifth stack. But I need my glasses which are in my bag. I'll be back in a minute.'

'What am I looking for?' Hilary asked.

'Look for Keble's name.'

Katherine moved sideways out of the stacks.

211

'I can't see anything,' Hilary said. 'I think I'm drunk.'

'Concentrate.' Katherine grasped the handle that made the stack move ponderously forward. Like two pieces of bread forming a sandwich round a filling, the gap closed between the fifth and sixth stack.

'Help!' Hilary yelled, dropping the book. It landed hard on her feet. 'Help!' She fell forward.

'For goodness sake, push,' Katherine said urgently to Moira. 'I haven't got enough pressure.'

'Oh my God! This wasn't part of the bargain. I've done my bit.'

'Help,' Hilary shouted, her voice muffled.

'We'll be in real trouble if she gets out. Push at the handle. We have to close them.'

Moira put her considerable weight behind Katherine and pushed the handle. Inch by inch the stack rolled shut.

Afterwards they closed all the stacks. The cleaners were unlikely to investigate; they would be grateful not to sweep between them. Until someone wished to consult *Crockford's Clerical Dictionary* they would remain shut. The Library was nearly empty, the long weekend acting like a siren's call. As it was summer and holiday time had started it might be some time before the stacks gave up their grizzly remains. At least Katherine hoped so.

Nobody noticed them re-enter the entrance hall, where Maisy was once more sitting safely in her chair, because everyone was watching Georgina being loaded into an ambulance. Georgina's left leg was unnaturally twisted to the right. She was in agony.

Chapter Fifteen

On March the 3rd, 1997 the Pearls met together in Katherine's flat.

Katherine opened the proceedings. 'As you know, Moira is not with us. Her heart, which has given her cause for fright in the past year, will not allow her to travel . . .'

Moira sits on her sunny terrace in Saint-Barthélemy. On a table beside her is her beloved rum and orange drink, the top sprouting greenery, half a slice of orange and two cherries. Her cat lies relaxed, half stretched on its back exposing its midriff to the morning sun. There is a book open on her lap but she is not reading. She is fingering a letter that she uses to keep her place in the novel. It is the one from Katherine she missed a year ago telling her of the lecture she was to give at the Literary Society and of the meeting planned for The Chaplet of Pearls. Moira often re-reads it. It is a message out of the past, light-headed with innocence and goodwill. She experiences a moment of drowning anguish. Whenever this happens, and it happens quite often, she thinks she is having a heart attack.

'. . . and Maisy was not able to make arrangements to come out from Acton . . .'

Maisy is in her wheelchair in the common room of St Theresa's Home for the Elderly and Infirm. She does not often think about the Pearls' behaviour in the London Library that afternoon. She is given pills to reduce the pain of her arthritis twice a day, and they make her a little woozy. Because she feels less pain, she is easier to handle when being dressed, undressed and washed, and she is less critical and difficult than when she arrived nine months ago. All this saves on staff time. When she does think about the fate of Hilary Greep she does not blame Katherine for her participation in it. She views the actions of the Pearls as a Midsummer Day's Madness.

'Portia has resigned from The Chaplet of Pearls and has suggested in a letter that it should be disbanded . . .'

Portia prays hourly. She wears only thin cotton. Her knobbly legs are bare and she wears sandals, longing for pneumonia and death. She takes no interest in Archie and Mrs Willis. How can she? She is unclean. A pollutant whose touch is slime. She would like to confess but to do so would bring anguish and shame on her children who innocently go about their lives raising lively, healthy and cheerful offspring. Portia will not allow her grandchildren to visit her in case she corrupts them, and Harry's shirts are now sent off to the laundry in Dulverton. In her great anger at herself and at Katherine, she would like to be placed in the dock. Most of all she would like to see Katherine in the dock, explaining their action to a sarcastic lawyer in front of a judge and jury. As Portia thinks this she writes to Katherine. Portia writes often to Katherine. Sometimes the letters plead with her to repent before Katherine is faced with hell. Other times she tells her she is the devil incarnate. She thinks a lot about Judas and how he could not believe in God's mercy. Can she?

214

'Their absence leaves us sadly depleted. It has been suggested, not only by Portia but also by Georgina, that perhaps the time has come to disband our group . . .'

It has taken a good deal of energy for Georgina to struggle out to this final meeting of the Pearls at Katherine's flat. She is in a wheelchair. The broken leg she sustained in the London Library that afternoon never healed. She is living on the fourth floor of a Victorian mansion block with porterage. Her children found the apartment while she was in hospital following complications with her leg. It was obvious that in her crippled state she could not manage in the Belgrave Square house. She has a male nurse to look after her. Georgio has disappeared. She is attending this last meeting of The Chaplet of Pearls for the sake of Grace. Both she and Katherine worry about Grace. Georgina finds it difficult to think back to their action on that day in the London Library. Afterwards she was so muzzy with pain and drugs that it now appears more like a dream than something in which she voluntarily took part. Convenient though this is, she only has to see or hear from Grace for the unendurable reality of the girl's death to flood her mind.

'So this will be our last meeting . . .'

Katherine no longer opens Portia's letters. She concentrates on what is containable. Possibly, Grace can be soothed and gentled with enough thought and effort. She owes her that effort. She no longer understands what drove her. How could she think she could arrest the passage of time by killing Hilary Greep? There will, of course, be other Hilary Greeps coming along. Katherine rarely relaxes; as she talks, reads, walks the Pekinese and lunches with Grace she sees herself in the basement turning the handle of the stacks to the muffled cries of Hilary Greep. She knows her guilt and

215

the vividness of her vision of events will fade. There surely will come a time when she will think, did I really do that? Did I murder Hilary Greep? All emotional and mental pain fades in the end – unless you are mad. Surely, Portia's will too. Unless she is mad.

'At this, our last meeting, it seems fitting that Grace read her inaugural paper to us. During the past year she has put in a great deal of study on the life of Charlotte M. Yonge. In fact she has probably concentrated more hours of study on her in the last nine months than the rest of the Pearls have in the years of our group's existence. She is now, without doubt, the greatest living expert and exponent on her life and works! She will address us on the subject of Fashion in the Charlotte M. Yonge Novel.' She looked benignly at the quivering Grace. Intellectually she had no difficulty with kindness.

Grace rose and settled in the chair facing Georgina and Katherine. She held two exercise books pressed to her breasts. One was red, the other green.

'Before I tell you about Fashion in Charlotte M. Yonge's Novels, I would like to touch on another aspect of her life. I would like to start with a description of Miss Yonge which I discovered during my researches.' She opened the green notebook at a marker. 'What I'm going to quote I found in A. R. Mowbray's *Glimpses of the Past* and is a letter from Elizabeth Wordsworth to Miss Frere about the opening of Keble College in 1870 when Miss Yonge was in late middle-age.' She read out, '"In the evening Pris, Susan and I agreed we would go to New College Chapel. We stopped at the Warden's first for a cup of tea. Miss Yonge (*the* Miss Yonge), who was, like ourselves, to be his guest, had just arrived, and went with us to the chapel. We had always been told she was shy, but I can only say, no one could have been pleasanter or more natural. She is a handsome woman; handsomer now, I dare say, because probably softer-looking than when younger. She looks and is Devonshire all over, with the most beautiful brown eyes, brunette colouring, brownish hands . . ."' (Grace started crying, but her voice held steady. She could not control what her eyes did, but she had practised for days to make sure that her voice held firm.) '". . . and plenty of white hair, which, contrasted with such a healthy complexion, makes her like the picture of some powdered, but not rouged, marquise of the *ancien régime* – an impression which is strengthened by her tall, plump, well-set-up figure. Her voice is peculiar. I suppose it is the way they talk down in Devonshire. Altogether she gives one a feeling of country, and out of doors, and looks as if she ought always to be giving you syllabubs out of beautiful old china in a nice old-fashioned garden." So you see,' Grace said, opening her arms wide and sobbing, 'we were quite right to kill her. This is the *real* Charlotte M. Yonge. This is how she really was . . .'

A NOTE ON THE AUTHOR

Harriet Waugh is the author of three previous novels, *Mirror, Mirror*, *Mother's Footsteps* and *Kate's House*. She reviews for the *Spectator* and lives in London.